PRAISE FOR *The Ca...*

"This arresting, heartbreaking, and meditati... of anxiety and shows how, though difficult... lead both to living one's best life and living life the best one can."
—*Booklist* (starred review)

"Hand this to anyone trying their best wobbling through the precarious and precious parts of life."
—*Bulletin of the Center for Children's Books* (starred review)

"An intriguing dynamic and a twist on the typical romance arc. Ocean's original narration and worldview are immersive and sympathetic."
—*Kirkus Reviews*

PRAISE FOR *This Is Where the World Ends*

"Zhang's effortless exploration of the complex intersection of memory and perception, and intricate, menace-laden plot is a perfect fit for fans of E. Lockhart's compelling *We Were Liars*."
—*Booklist* (starred review)

"This will make a great pairing with Laurie Halse Anderson's *Speak*."
—*Voice of Youth Advocates* (starred review)

"A dark, complicated tale, steeped in obsession [and] painful secrets. . . . This is most definitely a novel that will have fans talking."
—*Kirkus Reviews*

PRAISE FOR *Falling into Place*

An Indies Introduce Title

A Top Ten Indie Next Pick

"The breezy yet powerful and exceptionally perceptive writing style, multifaceted characters, surprisingly hopeful ending, and pertinent contemporary themes frame an engrossing, thought-provoking story."
—*School Library Journal*

AMY ZHANG

THE CARTOGRAPHERS

Greenwillow Books
An Imprint of HarperCollins*Publishers*

The Cartographers

Copyright © 2023 by Amy Zhang

All rights reserved. No part of this book may be used or reproduced in any manner whatsoever without written permission except in the case of brief quotations embodied in critical articles and reviews. Printed in the United States of America. For information address HarperCollins Children's Books, a division of HarperCollins Publishers, 195 Broadway, New York, NY 10007.

www.epicreads.com

The text of this book is set in 12-point Garamond 3.

Book design by Paul Zakris

Library of Congress Cataloging-in-Publication Data

Names: Zhang, Amy, author. Title: The cartographers / Amy Zhang.
Description: First edition. |
New York, NY : Greenwillow Books, an imprint of HarperCollins Publishers, [2022] |
Audience: Ages 14 up. | Audience: Grades 10-12. |
Summary: Seventeen-year-old Ocean Sun moves to New York City to start college, but she defers her enrollment, keeping it a secret from her immigrant mother, and instead uses the time to deal with her ambivalence about her place in the world.
Identifiers: LCCN 2022008241 (print) | LCCN 2022008242 (ebook) |
ISBN 9780062383082 (paperback) | ISBN 9780062383099 (ebook)
Subjects: CYAC: Suicide—Fiction. | Depression, Mental—Fiction. | Philosophy—Fiction. |
Chinese Americans—Fiction. | New York (N.Y.)—Fiction. | LCGFT: Novels.
Classification: LCC PZ7.1.Z5 Car 2022 (print) | LCC PZ7.1.Z5 (ebook) | DDC [Fic]—dc23
LC record available at https://lccn.loc.gov/2022008241
LC ebook record available at https://lccn.loc.gov/2022008242

23 24 25 26 27 LBC 5 4 3 2 1

First Greenwillow paperback edition, 2024

GREENWILLOW BOOKS

For my parents and grandparents

There is not a single human being
who does not despair at least a little.
—SØREN KIERKEGAARD,
Fear and Trembling and the Sickness Unto Death

IF YOU GIVE A RAT A COFFEE

On the subway, I worried I was already dead. Everything about New York City transit felt like the afterlife—not hell but some kind of middle place, where all the trains ran late or stalled between stations. I had only been living in the city for a month, but for thirty days straight I saw things on the subway that made me dizzy with vertigo: men in loose boots pole dancing in crowded cars, dogs dressed in twenty-gallon grocery bags, pigeons that boarded without paying the fare. No one looked me in the face, and every rat on the platform knew its way better than I did.

The feeling was worse late at night and in unfamiliar stations. Now, alone, higher up in Manhattan than I'd ever been before, I knew for certain I was dead. It was well past midnight. I was alone because my roommates had gone home to hook up with each other. Or so I had heard—neither had bothered to tell me they were leaving. I was only uptown because my roommate Georgie, the occasional comedian, had scored a gig at a decrepit bar and dragged us with her for moral support. But the show ended without Georgie ever taking the stage. I searched the bar for half an hour before another comedian told me Georgie had gotten so jittery that Tashya, my other roommate, had to make out with her in the bathroom until the two of them disappeared into the night. It didn't surprise me, exactly. The sexual tension between them had been thick enough to cut with a plastic knife.

There was no telling when the next train would come. The electronic display was down. It was a shabby station, and most of the light bulbs were broken, which made everything barely dimensional. There was no one else on the platform. I looked down to the tracks and saw a rat dragging a cup of coffee across the third rail. Though the rat should have been thoroughly electrocuted, it bore on stubbornly. I thought, *That's it, I've died.* Both the rat and I were dead. I felt full of despair, to be infinite in the subway.

"Hey. *Hey!*"

I jumped. Then I looked up and saw a boy across the tracks, on the uptown platform. He was outrageously tall and waving both his arms.

"Hey!" he called again. "The trains are down."

I blinked. What little light there was refracted strangely off the grimy surfaces. Waving as he was, the boy looked exactly like a wind turbine. It was so surreal.

"What?" My voice was raspy. For sure I was dead.

"The trains!" he bellowed, like he was several hundred yards away instead of maybe fifty. Then he held up a finger—*wait*—and ran back through the turnstiles, then disappeared up the stairs. A minute later I heard footsteps thundering back down, and then he was jumping the turnstile on my side of the station. My stomach dropped to my feet.

"The trains," he said. He wasn't out of breath at all. "They're not running."

He was much taller now that he was close, looming over me. There was a crackling sound from the tracks. I looked down to see the rat struggling to pull the coffee cup through a crevice.

"I heard you," I said. "I meant, like . . . what?"

"No trains," he insisted. "The power's down. Look." He pointed to the train display, as if it were normally a reliable source of information. "The whole city's blacked out. You don't know? How long have you been waiting here? Haven't you seen the sky?"

Nothing he said made any sense. The sky? I had no idea how long I'd been waiting—somewhere between five and forty-five minutes. My sense of time was abysmal even under normal circumstances.

"You have to come see," he said, extending a hand. I didn't move. His hand hung there between us, preposterously larger than mine. I wasn't going to follow him anywhere, this stranger with his strings of words that meant nothing at all. I glanced again at the display.

He let his hand drop. He scratched the back of his head. "Okay, I get it, I'm coming off a bit strong, huh? I'm not a creep, I swear."

"You should get that tattooed," I said. "The creep motto."

He laughed. His laugh surprised me: unabashed and echoing across the empty station, as though I were not a stranger but a friend.

"I guess that's true," he said. The laugh was still on his face. I gathered my courage and looked directly at him for the first time, though only for a second, so that I got a smattering of impressions rather than a good look: strong eyebrows and high cheekbones and a wide forehead, planar and strange. His nose was crooked, but his teeth were very straight. He was wearing a black windbreaker that was too big, even on him.

"Look," he said, "my name's Constantine Brave."

"No way," I blurted. "That's an awful fake name. Worse than Joe Alibi. Worse than John Smith."

He threw up his hands. All his movements seemed like this: sudden and a little jerky. I thought of Don Quixote, baffled by windmills and giants. "No, I swear, it's my real name. Most people call me Constant, and some people just call me Brave, but you can call me whatever you want. What's your name?"

I felt like I'd walked into a trap, though I hadn't asked for his name in the first place, or asked him to come to my side of the station. "Ocean," I said, eventually, when I could think of no way around it. "My name's Ocean Sun."

He didn't accuse me of making it up, though he could have, since Ocean Sun is not empirically more or less ridiculous than Constantine Brave. He only nodded, and repeated it several times. "Ocean, Ocean, Ocean." Like an incantation. It sounded strange in his voice, almost unfamiliar; I was worried I'd forget to answer somehow if he ever called me, like it was fake after all. "It's good to meet you, Ocean. And now you must come see something extraordinary."

I peered at him, or rather at a spot on his chin that I didn't feel so afraid to look at directly. The lights in the station were difficult to see by—emergency lights, I realized, on their own little generator. My stomach suddenly felt hollow. I couldn't remember a single thing I knew for certain.

"Are you dead too?" I asked.

"What?"

"Never mind," I said. "What's so extraordinary?"

I followed Constant—*Constant*, the inconsistent, who appeared from thin air—out of the train station and felt powerfully that I was dreaming. His body blocked out everything but the two feet or so directly in front of me. I had some fuzzy peripherals but no aerial awareness at all, since he had probably a foot and a half on me. On the narrow subway steps, he made me claustrophobic.

Over his shoulder he said, "Want to hear me sing, Eurydice?" Then he winked at me and tapped the right side of his nose, thrice.

"Please don't," I said. I felt a little nauseous and sent a prayer to anyone listening that he was not a human trafficker or on serious drugs. "Anyway, you looked back."

He laughed. "Don't disappear on me, Ocean." But he didn't look back again to check.

Then we were outside, and something was wrong with the light. It took me a long time to realize that all the lights were *off*: the streetlights and the signs and all the windows in all the buildings. There were only headlights, occasionally, feeling their way through the dark. The colors were gone; everything was strange and flat, and fading out of existence once we passed, scenery on a treadmill.

"Turn around," said Constant.

And then: the extraordinary thing. I turned to face the east, where the sky was incandescent. There was a vivid light on the horizon, as though a star had crashed somewhere in Queens. The sky above the borough was bright and ghost blue.

"Holy shit," I said, the only thing I could think of to say.

"Is that extraordinary or what?" he said. He sounded awfully cheerful, though it looked like the end of the world.

I felt frantic. What was it? What had happened? Of

course a star hadn't crashed into the earth, but could it be a small asteroid? Was it a bomb? Was it nuclear fallout? I couldn't remember anything about nuclear fallout, except that you should skip conditioning your hair. Was it aliens? The intense fluorescent blue coming from Queens didn't seem quite of this earth.

"What is that?" My voice was very high.

"I guess there's an electric fire at a power station. The transformer exploded or something like that—"

"A nuclear plant?"

"No, just a regular power grid station," he said. He gave me a strange look. "I think they have it under control now, but you know." He windmilled his arms again. "No power." When I didn't say anything, he went on. "Are you okay? How long were you sitting down there? What train were you waiting for? Do you have a way home? Is it too far to walk?"

The way he asked all his questions at once made me feel like my head was being slapped right off my neck. Worse, all his questions were uncomfortable.

"How long is the power going to be down?" My voice was still at a loftier octave than I could ever remember hearing it. "When do you think the train's going to be running again?"

"Probably not for a while. Can you call a rideshare?"

I could not call a rideshare. I began to panic. There were

no trains, and I was probably fifteen miles away from the apartment, which meant I was stranded, and I didn't know a single person, place, or thing that could help me, except this bizarre person Constant, who despite his name had come from nowhere at all and seemed liable to disappear in just the same way.

THE BAD PLACE

I couldn't call a rideshare because it might expose an enormous lie upon which my entire existence depended.

There were also several smaller but equally important reasons. My phone was dead. Even if it weren't, my bank card had only nineteen dollars and thirty-four cents on it as of this morning—certainly not enough for a car, or a hotel. I had an emergency credit card, but the card company texted my mother promptly after each transaction, and I was desperate to avoid the scenario in which my mother called to ask me why I needed a car to Brooklyn when, as far as she knew, I ought to be asleep in a dorm room.

The truth was I had deferred my college acceptance by a year. When I'd first visited the college after my acceptance, I'd seen seven people sobbing hysterically on the library steps, and I'd gone home with a dozen different pamphlets on mental health. I wasn't suicidal, I told myself, or at least I wasn't yet.

Later that summer I decided to defer. Considering the scale of the whole fraudulent operation, it was shockingly easy to pull off—all I really had to do was send out a few emails. By some miracle I'd amassed enough in scholarships to cover my entire tuition, but the various foundations were more than happy to put off their charity for another year, and the admissions office cared even less. Even making my own living arrangements, the idea of which had given me serious insomnia for the last month of the summer, ended up being something I was able to resolve over a few days. There were plenty of places that wouldn't rent to me because I had no credit score or cosigner, but there were just as many places already inhabited by two or three, or even six or seven people, who were just desperate to fill a room before next month's rent was due. It only took a few hours, and I was set to live with a self-described "comedian stargirl" named Georgie and a stern-looking conservatory student named Tashya, who was from Slovenia. That was all I could find out about her online—that she was from Slovenia. Her social media gave away nothing else, not what instrument she played or who she was friends with or even how old she was, which I thought was really weird until I felt obsessive, like I was the weird one, stalking a stranger across five different social media platforms. Anyway, when I met her, the first thing she told me was that she played piano.

Now I was here, and everything was happening very fast. It made me dizzy. Though the fraud had slipped out of my head and exactly into place, it seemed constantly on the brink of collapse. I had a perpetual pinched feeling above my sternum, like my whole life was about to lurch out of my grasp, like it didn't belong to me.

I couldn't call a rideshare.

"Hey, look, I can call you a rideshare," said Constant, when I had been quiet for too long. My stomach plunged. He said it like it was nothing, and I didn't know if was an empty offer, or if he was really just nonchalant about a seventy-dollar rideshare that could easily surge to three digits on a night like this. I didn't like what either might say about him.

"No," I blurted, so fast it was rude. But my mother had drilled these two things into me: that honesty was better than dishonesty, and that it was better to give a gift than to receive one. Gifts had to be reciprocated; they carried expectation and aged like debt. You should never accept a gift you could not afford for yourself, just like you should never give a gift to prove a point. I couldn't bear the idea of accepting a rideshare from this stranger with the absurd name. Besides, I didn't want him to have my address.

But I also couldn't think of what else to do. I could wait in the station until the trains were running again, as they were bound to, eventually. But now that I was outside in the uncanny blue air, the idea of waiting downstairs in the dark was unbearable. If I knew the city better, or if my phone weren't dead, I could try to walk to my apartment, which would probably take all night and which I was frightened to do for obvious reasons and because I hated when rats swarmed out from the mountains of trash. Also, it was a hopeless endeavor without a map.

I was paralyzed with indecision, like maybe if I stood still for long enough everything might oblige by sorting itself out. Constant was watching me with his hands in his pockets. He didn't seem all that perturbed that I'd snapped at him and was perfectly content to watch me struggle. I was reaching a critical level in the amount of emotion I could take in at once, and I was sure to snap again, or cry, if he kept looking at me like that, so calmly.

"Or I'll walk with you," he said. "If you want."

My mouth was already opening to say no. I wasn't sure I wanted the company, but I did seem to need it, phoneless and so late at night. It was still a gift he was offering, but at least it seemed to both our disadvantages. I could lose him at any time, I told myself, if he turned out to be annoying.

"It's a pretty long walk," I said slowly.

He shrugged. "I don't mind."

I took a good look at him. I didn't shy away from his eyes this time. They were wide and greenish, as strange and liminal as the rest of him. I didn't know who he was or where he'd come from, but at least, out of the two of us, he knew where he was going.

The apartment I rented with Tashya and Georgie was in Brooklyn—thirteen point six miles away, four hours and fifty minutes by foot. Constant was sure we could do it in less. "I'm a fast walker," he said. "The GPS always underestimates me."

But I was still wary. What were we supposed to say to each other for four hours and fifty minutes? I wasn't a fast walker—my legs weren't nearly as long as his.

Then we were off. For the first few minutes I said nothing. All I could do was stare at the sky. I felt the unnatural light in my ears and my chest. The distant billowing smoke caused the terrible and beautiful blue to move like an aurora borealis. Beneath it, the city was balmy and illuminated, the best of summer in New York. I had learned this from Georgie— that deep night was the only bearable time during the wet heat of New York City summer, rat season, which lasted well into October or even, recently, November. Georgie had lived here all her life and detested every season: rat, construction, Seasonal Affective Disorder, and allergy. It was part of the comedy set she'd failed to perform.

But Constant couldn't keep quiet for long. "So what brings you so far uptown, Brooklyn girl?"

I was startled. "I'm not really from Brooklyn," I said, feeling like I'd tricked him.

"Okay," he said cheerfully. Everything about him had that loping cheerfulness, even the way he walked. He strode with his hands in his pockets and a certain buoyancy, like he was less prone to gravity than me. "So where are you from then, Ocean Sun?"

The question made me the opposite of cheerful. I didn't know how to answer it. I hated when people asked, because they might have meant any number of things: where I'd moved from or where I'd emigrated from or where I was born, where my parents grew up or where their parents lived and died, where I'd arrived and where I called home and whether I was ever leaving. Sometimes the question was friendly and sometimes it was not, and it was almost impossible to know what he meant.

"I don't know," I said. Even I could hear how despairing I sounded. "Where are *you* from?"

"Jersey, mostly," said Constant. "But now I live up here, for school."

We kept walking. I got that feeling again, like the city was disappearing behind me as soon as I'd passed by, and the skyscrapers ahead were being rendered just as we approached them. I felt like I was dreaming. There were so many things I didn't understand. Who had built the skyscrapers, and how? Who was Constantine to appear like Virgil in this infernal city?

"So," said Constant, "are you like a ghost, or what?"

"What?"

"It's cool if you are," he said. "I don't mind. No questions asked."

I was so tired. I'd slept better since I'd arrived in Brooklyn with all my lies intact, but I was still tired all the time. I could feel the hours of sleep I'd lost this summer hanging over me like a thick, wet weight.

"But you've already asked so many questions" was all I could think of to say.

"Oh," he said, and reflected on this briefly. "Well, starting now." He seemed to mean it.

I felt suddenly terrible to disappoint him—to say that there was no quest or departure from the ordinary, that this was not a beginning. I couldn't be sure if I was dead or alive, but either way I was unextraordinary.

"I'm not dead," I said, but I didn't sound all that convincing, even to myself.

"Oh," he said, and paused. "Oh, okay. It's just that when I saw you in the station, you asked me if I was dead too, so I guess I assumed. I'm not either, by the way."

"Not what?"

"Dead," he said. "I'm also still alive. I guess we're short on the supernatural element tonight. It's the sky. The light makes everything seem a little bizarre. But why did you think *I* was dead? And why *too*?"

I couldn't believe I'd been worried that the walk would be silent and awkward. This onslaught of questions was much worse. He was relentless. "I thought you were done with the questions," I said.

"Yeah, out of respect for your passing. But curiosity is the first sign of life, my friend. So what's going on here? Why are you stranded in the middle of the night? Are you running toward or running from? Are you throwing something incriminating into the river? Are you trying to get a look at the coyote at Central Park? Because I am too. Are you under any influences? Wait."

He stopped and squinted at me. All at once he was serious; it was the first time I'd seen his strange face without that persistent cheer. His eyes were piercing. They seemed to pin me in place, like I was taxidermized.

"You weren't doing anything stupid, were you?" he said. "Because death by third rail has got to be the worst way to die. Well, specifically death by pissing on the third rail. Did you know all six hundred volts go up the stream of your urine and zaps you right in the—"

"No!" I hadn't been there to jump onto the third rail, though of course I had thought about it, sitting there in the strange and blurry dark. Sometimes, in some moods, I couldn't stand on any sort of raised thing—a platform or a scenic tower or a bridge—without wanting to jump. After all, how else could I check if I was already dead?

"No," I said again, and when he kept squinting at me, I added more waspishly, "Sorry, not your flight risk. Or ghost, or whoever else you look to for an adventure."

"I'm the flight risk, I think," he said, so matter-of-factly it didn't occur to me until later to ask what he meant. But the awkwardness had passed, and we started walking again. "So what the hell did you do in your past life, to wind up at the 125th Street station in the afterlife?"

"Nothing," I said.

And this was exactly the problem. I'd been alive for nearly eighteen years, and I didn't have anything to show for it. It seemed I hadn't accomplished much at all. For my whole life, my mother had impressed upon me the importance of getting admitted to a good college—so I'd done the requisite extracurriculars and advanced placement classes and even a few low-contact sports. But then I got accepted—and it was so anticlimactic that I felt both that I'd worked toward a scam, and like I had nothing else to work for at all. I deflated like a balloon. Any motivation I'd ever had fled so quickly I wasn't even sure I could even remember how it felt in the first place.

"Isn't that what most people do?" I continued. "You do some good things and some horrible things, but mostly you do self-serving things, and before you know it, your whole life has gone by and you have nothing to show for it."

"And that isn't tragedy?" His voice was perfectly neutral—I couldn't tell what he was thinking at all. It was too dark and he was too tall for me to see his face. Our pace had slowed; we were wading through a block of rustling, overflowing trash. Things had grown more nightmarish, not less.

"It's not good, either," I said. "It's just—meaningless. But people aren't motivated by purpose, I think. Not most of the time, not most people. Most people are motivated by comfort, and security."

"Huh," said Constant. "I disagree." But he didn't say anything else, as if he thought that was enough. In a way it was, because I liked that he was unafraid to have an opinion. Having opinions intimidated me: defending them, staying consistent to them, admitting you were wrong about them.

We passed another subway station. Constant stopped walking. He stopped so abruptly I smacked straight into his back. He was as tall and solid as a wall. I bounced off and almost fell to the curb.

"Speaking of self-serving things," he said. "Do you mind if we stop at this station for just a few minutes? I have to go back down for, ah—something. But I promise it'll be quick."

I was wary. "Why?"

"I don't care about good or horrible things," he said. "I don't care about self-serving things either. I just want to do something that lasts."

This station was completely dark. On the way down the stairs we turned a corner and suddenly there was only the faint red light of the exits and the distant, ambient blinking coming from the tunnels. Constant turned on the flashlight on his phone, which didn't help much. Everything looked bizarre and lacking in perspective, like a video game with ancient graphics. I couldn't see obstacles—poles, turnstiles, gates—until I nearly ran into them. So I inched along, worried I'd launch myself off the platform and straight onto the tracks. This seemed like exactly where Constant was headed. He walked to the edge of the platform and stood there looking down.

Then he spun around to face me again. "Look," he said, and opened his enormous windbreaker. He held it wide open but didn't take care to point the light, so I couldn't see what he was showing me.

"Oh, sorry," he said. "Wait, I have another flashlight." He rummaged around, then extended something toward me in the dark.

"It's heavy," he warned.

Nonetheless I dropped it. It was the size and shape of a brick. It fell right through my hands and crashed to the ground, where it began to scream. The high, shrill beeps filled the station. It flooded me with dread.

"Ah, shit," said Constant. He bent to inspect the loud flashlight. He fumbled with it for long minutes while I shifted from foot to foot in the dark. I hadn't realized how closely I'd been listening for the scutter of rats or the footsteps of murderers until all of a sudden I could hear nothing but the flashlight. Then, just as suddenly, it went silent, and I was blinded by light.

"Shit," Constant said again, and swung the light away. I was still seeing stars. When I looked at his face, there was only a ball of light, like a Magritte painting. The light was so bright that when Constant pointed it down the platform I could see all the way into the tunnel; it was bright as an incoming train.

"It's a Geiger counter," said Constant.

"Pardon?"

"The flashlight," he said, waving it; the light swerved violently. "I mean, it's a flashlight, obviously. But it's also a Soviet-era Geiger counter. Look." He held it toward me, butt first. I had to blink several more times for my vision to clear enough that I could see a dense block of Cyrillic print, and above it an ominous meter with a single twitching needle.

"I think it's just old," said Constant. "I don't think there's radioactive sludge in here."

The Geiger counter let out a final whine of complaint, to remind us we could never be sure. We looked at it dubiously.

But in its light I could finally see the inside of Constant's enormous windbreaker. His waistband was lined with cans of spray paint: vivid blue, tomato red, lime green. My stomach sank. I wondered if I'd ever make it back to Brooklyn. Constant shot me a wicked grin. He spun around and launched himself off the platform, onto the tracks, so fast I couldn't even scream.

"No time to tag like a citywide blackout," he said. "You coming?"

I peered over the edge. He was standing right in the gutter of the track; at his feet, I saw torn Takis bags and plastic bottles and rotting fruit and puddles of human and animal urine. I felt my gag reflex changing the shape of my nose. Constant, if it was possible, grinned harder. He offered me a hand.

I didn't take it. "I don't like rats."

"Who does? They won't hurt us."

His hand hung awkwardly between us.

"Don't you trust me?" he asked.

I really didn't. My confidence had fled into the dark. "Why do you have a Soviet Geiger counter?" I asked. "Do you do this a lot, this whole graffiti artist shtick?"

"You mean, do I bring girls into dark subway stations and seduce them with my artistic prowess?"

"Do you?"

"If you come, you'd be the first," he said. "Jump. I'll catch you."

I didn't jump. I sat down on the yellow line, the bumpy platform digging into the backs of my thighs, and slid slowly down. I felt full of repulsion, or fear, or panic, or excitement. There was a knot in my throat. My heart was beating very fast. I didn't trust him, but I had already followed him all this way; what was I supposed to do—turn back? I slid off the edge. But the distance was farther than I'd thought, and halfway down, when my feet still hadn't hit toxic sludge, I made a choked little noise not unlike the Geiger counter.

His arms came around me, solid and stronger than I expected. I yelped again. I was against his chest with the Geiger counter poking chunkily into my back; he was the largest person I'd ever been in physical contact with, and I had a bizarre sense that in his arms I looked like an altogether different species of human. His mouth was briefly, conspicuously close to mine.

Then he set me on my feet. "Sorry," he said. "You were about to land in a puddle."

"It's okay." But I sounded squeaky and breathless, and I didn't know where to look. I focused on the spray paint cans in his waistband. Bright orange, sunflower yellow, slate gray.

"What are you going to paint?" I asked.

He grinned again: wicked, crooked, wide. He motioned for me to follow him. We went onward, into the dark.

The New York subway system has more stations than any other transit system in the world, and they operated twenty-four hours a day, seven days a week—at least theoretically. All of this made it just about the most difficult place to innovate, or clean. The tracks were extraordinarily dirty. I was terrified.

I was sure I could hear rats, their nails scratching closer to us. I couldn't believe we were in the developed world. The flashlight caused wavering shadows, and it was difficult to tell what were rodents, what was loose trash, and what were worse things living in the dark. I was almost jogging to keep up with Constant, who seemed entirely unperturbed by the grime, like he had done this many times before.

As I scrambled after him, he told me about the Geiger counter. His father was a nuclear engineer and his grandfather was a hoarder, and all his life his apartment had been filled with Geiger counters that his grandfather found in Eastern European pawn shops and brought home as gifts. They had Geiger counters from Ukraine, Poland, the Czech Republic, Slovakia, Hungary, Slovenia, Romania, and Serbia. "He had this idea that my dad collects them," Constant said, "which I guess he does now. And now my grandfather is dead, so we have to keep all the Geiger counters. Sentimentality really complicates everything, doesn't it?"

"Are there cameras down here?" I asked. "Should we cover our faces?"

He tried not to laugh. Immediately I felt terrible. It would have been better if he'd laughed outright—I felt more humiliated that he tried to hide it. "The power's down," he reminded me. "But we're just going a little farther. If there's a train outside the station, we'll tag that. If not, we'll just tag a wall."

"A train?"

"Sure," he said. "Everywhere under this city, the trains must be stuck on their tracks. They'll be evacuated by now. A golden opportunity, Ocean. It may never happen again in our lifetimes."

I was startled to hear him say my name. I realized I hadn't said his yet, aloud.

He stopped all of a sudden. "Alas, no trains here tonight, I think. It's okay. We'll do this wall. The good thing about the subway tunnels is that they're all already covered in paint. You never want to tag a blank wall, Ocean, and you never want to cover someone else's artwork. Other than that, you can do anything you want. What color?"

"What?"

"What color do you want?" he asked. "You can have the red, if you want, since it's your first time. For luck."

He offered me his hip, jutting toward me so the red can glared at me. I took a step back and almost fell over. "I think I'll just watch."

"Sure," said Constant. "Next time, then."

He shook his can vigorously, and then began to paint.

For several long minutes I couldn't make out what he was painting. He seemed to be blocking out large areas in beige—odd, blobby shapes that didn't resemble numbers or letters. I kept watching and watching and feeling more unmoored, unable to recognize a single thing. Then he painted another stroke, and all of a sudden I knew what he was painting.

"That's New York," I said. "That's the city." Suddenly it was obvious. There was Manhattan, and Brooklyn, and Queens. He finished the South Bronx and added Central Park. The map was enormous. In another few minutes it looked done to me: he'd painted Prospect Park and Washington Square Park and the East and Hudson Rivers; there was the Brooklyn Bridge and the Manhattan Bridge and Williamsburg Bridge; he added beaches across the bottom of Brooklyn and at the Rockaways, and then Governors Island and Roosevelt Island and Staten Island. But he wasn't done. He shaded in light topographies and added smaller, square parks. He firmed up the edges of the islands and adjusted the shape of the financial district.

Then he stood back and squinted at it. He was perfectly still for several minutes. Down the tunnel, I saw two rats break from a hole in the wall and sprint across the tracks, their tails streaking behind them.

"And now the fun begins," said Constant. He pulled out a vivid blue canister with a narrow tip. "What I usually do is start with the longest line," he said. He shook the canister several times and held it high above his head, at the highest tip of Manhattan. "That's the A, which goes thirty-two miles from Inwood to the Rockaways." He sprayed a thin line down the west side of the island, across and down Brooklyn, to the narrow isle at the bottom of the wall. The blue line was smooth and stern, and followed all the right swerves; he didn't once hesitate, and the line didn't falter. Watching him, I really did feel more faith in the transit system than I had my whole time in the city.

"Isn't that wild?" he said. "Can you imagine that, building thirty-two miles of track? Then I add in the C and the E." The three blue lines converged in Manhattan but split at both ends, like braids unraveling. "When they were designing the subway map, the one they have now in all the stations and train cars and websites, one of the artists rode every single line with his eyes closed and drew the curves and lurches in the routes blind. It's a very poetic idea, but when I tried to do it, this extremely small angry girl tried to steal my headphones."

"From your ears?"

"No, from my lap. I had them out so I could hear the conductor."

"But if there are already maps in the trains and the stations, why vandalize the tunnels?" I asked.

"Because my maps are better," he said simply. "And good maps outlast bad ones. Look."

He started on the next-longest line, the F, which was bright orange, and around it added the B, D, and M. "The problem with the maps now is that they put all the local and express lines under the same color, and don't separate out the different routes. It's a terrible system. New York is full of terrible systems, but it's also full of people trying to make them better. Like us." He quirked an eyebrow and motioned the canister at me. I shook my head. I was sure I'd ruin his map. "Still no? All right, you can do the stations, if you want, after. Those are just dots. Anyway, it's not really that much more trouble to draw all the lines. But the transit authority won't do it and they won't let anyone else do it. Hence the vandalism."

I couldn't tell if he genuinely meant the things he said or if it was all talk. He really liked to paint the maps on subway cars, he said—"On them, inside them, it doesn't matter: that's where most people see it, and share it, and use it"—but of course this was also the most logistically difficult to execute. Inside the tunnels, the risk was lower, but so was the reward. "It's a good place to practice, though. I can almost always do a whole map in under thirty minutes now."

The red stretching far into the Bronx and into Brooklyn, the green making its efficient way, the yellow splitting toward the beaches. I knew the whole of the city was only three hundred square miles, but it was like he was painting the world and everyone in it. This was where I lived now, there was my life on the wall of a subway tunnel, put there by someone I didn't even know.

His phone died in my hand. We rearranged ourselves so that I could hold the Geiger counter while he added in detail, and as he was handing the light to me his features came together, all at once. Suddenly I knew his face, could see it in my head if I closed my eyes, could pick him out of a lineup or a crowd. I'd never forget it again. I realized that I really did like it, the quirk of his eyebrows and the hollows of his cheeks and the great plane of his forehead. When it came together it had this aesthetic quality, like his face was something he curated.

"What?" he asked. "Why are you staring at me?"

"I'm not," I said, and he grinned as I felt my cheeks grow hot. He turned back to the wall. My hand shook; the light from the Geiger counter wavered and the train lines seemed to move, uptown or downtown, toward Manhattan or away from it. Every few seconds I looked at his face again; I couldn't help it. Every time I looked I found something new I liked, as if it had appeared from nowhere. I liked the fullness of his bottom lip and the shape of his jaw. I liked his strange hairline and the way the hair fell into his eyes and I liked the way his face was a bit asymmetrical, unevenly divided by a slanting nose. *Constantine Brave,* I thought, again and again, until the words rearranged by themselves: Constantine the Brave.

"You want to do the last line?" he said, just as I blurted, "I was thinking about jumping, a little bit."

"What?" he said.

"What?" I said.

This was the problem with deciding not to kill yourself. After you tried once, the idea stuck there like a hangnail.

But if life was like a burning house—if the air became black with smoke and the ceiling was collapsing and living there became unbearable—you could always walk out the door. No one could ever blame you. You'd never keep a lobster from jumping out of a boiling pot, unless you planned to eat it.

He looked at me squarely. His face had changed again: his angular, robust features were as prone to severity as they were to cheerfulness. He made me feel scolded, though he'd said nothing at all. I was mortified. I couldn't believe the words had just come out of my mouth. What kind of person walked around announcing to strangers that they had suicidal ideations? I did not think well of suicidal people, and I was sure no one else did either. I felt depressed by this, that Constant might not think well of me. I had never told anyone so directly, not Georgie or Tashya, not my own mother. No one but Constantine Brave, here beneath the city.

"I thought I was already dead," I reminded him.

"Why's that?" he asked. "How many times have you almost died?"

I couldn't answer. He was still staring at me in that hard, stern way. I squirmed. I wondered if he knew his face could do that, make people squirm, if he practiced it.

"Look," he said, "I know. I know, okay? It's all just awful, isn't it? Just the concept of it all. You wake up and go to school even though having a degree hardly helps you get a job anymore, and then you wake up and go to your job that pays too little to repay the loans you needed to go to school in the first place, and every day you have to do all these tedious little things like wash your face and unload the dishwasher and squish into ancient subway cars with a thousand strangers. All of it's exhausting, and none of it even matters. It's all meaningless, the ways we keep ourselves busy on our rock circling our sun in what must be, like, the backwater of the universe."

Suddenly I felt like I might cry. "It's kind of a bad place," I said.

"Just awful," he agreed, and grinned at me. "And it's still better than nothing at all."

How did he know? How could he, for sure?

"Is it?" I asked.

"I think so," he said. He handed me the last canister of paint: light slate gray, for the shuttle between Grand Central and Times Square.

I took it, slowly. It was still warm from his hand. I shook it a few times, half-heartedly, so the pea bounced reluctantly inside.

"Straight and true, right across," said Constant. "Sometimes you just have to see where life takes you, even if it takes you to an unfortunate place."

"Like into the bowels of the city?"

"Especially the bowels of the city."

I shook the can again, with a little more conviction. The tinny noise ricocheted down the tunnels. It came back to us, carried on another, deeper rumbling.

We froze, like rats.

"Turn the flashlight off," said Constant. I clicked the Geiger counter and blinked hard, surprised by the sudden absence of light, the way it swallowed the whole world, all at once.

The rumbling continued, not close but not very far. We were not completely in the dark. Down the tunnels, like jewels, were red and green signal lights, and behind us, the lights from the station. The power was back on.

"Oh, fuck," said Constant, and turned to me. He put his hands on my shoulders and spun me toward the station lights. "Listen, Ocean. You and me, we have to run, okay? Ready?"

"What?" I yelped.

He shoved me forward. "Go!"

I lunged forward, only just caught myself, and sprinted. I had to, because Constant was right on my heels, and he was very fast. We ran. I hadn't run so fast since I was small, pumping furiously for the last leg of an elementary mile. It didn't feel like I was running from anything, because Constant was so close and enormous behind me that he may as well have been the world, but I must have known that we were about to be crushed flat by a train. My heart was in my throat and beating against my eardrums. There were flurries of movement at my feet: the rats too seemed to know something had changed, that the respite was over, that the city would never be so dark again. I had a terrible vision of landing on one as I ran, its body bursting like a juice box beneath my toes.

Finally Constant hoisted me up the service ladder and onto the ridge of the tunnel, along which we ran the last several feet until, at last, we were back in the station. He dragged me to a bench and we collapsed onto it just as a train whooshed by, running and running past us, until it had disappeared out the other end of the station. It didn't stop.

"Well," said Constant, panting, "maybe you can catch the next one."

We slid down on the bench until we were slumped against each other, my shoulder against his. I was suddenly, hideously aware of my body. I was sweating, and breathing so hard I was dizzy, but I couldn't pull my sprawled, clammy limbs in. I was still catching my breath, heaving lungfuls of subway air. I liked the feeling of it, the breath in my body. My arm was against his arm. And then all I could think about was his arm, which was so much longer and broader and firmer than mine. My breathing, no matter how I concentrated on it, refused to slow.

"I'd like a copy of your map," I said to him, eventually, when I could.

"Sure," he said. "It's twenty for the PDF, or fifty for an eight-by-eleven print, and ten dollars more if you want me to mat it. Plus shipping."

"Oh," I said. "Well, all right—"

"I'm kidding," he said. "Give me your email, I'll send it over to you."

He grinned at me. It was so companionable; it was nice to sit there with him, alive. The station was just as grim and dirty as before, but now, several hundred yards away, there was a spot we'd slathered in paint, better for us having been there. I felt relief, welling like tears. Could Constant be right—that this was not the afterlife? The tedium was not eternal yet. He pulled out a marker and rolled up his windbreaker to offer me the wide space of his forearm. My breath caught. I gave him my email.

"Cool," he said happily, rolling his sleeve back down. "So what now?"

What now? The great question. My breath rushed forth again, like a dam had broken. I flushed with vertigo; my head spun and began to throb with lack of sleep.

"What time is it?" I asked.

"Four in the morning exactly," said Constant.

This filled me with dread. The unluckiest time, a malevolent hour. In Chinese the word *four* sounds like the word *death*, a coincidence that fills the number with awful luck. I was superstitious in a visceral way, and shivered whenever

I saw someone wearing a white hat or stepping firmly on a sidewalk crack. I thought it was better to err on the side of caution. To be anywhere but the safety of my bed at four in the morning seemed like taunting fate.

"I guess I should take the next train that comes," I said, although I didn't exactly want to leave, either.

Constant didn't say anything. I was afraid to look at him. I was afraid to find him relieved, glad to see me go. It worried me that part of me hoped he would ask me to stay.

"Okay," he said. "The adventure continues another day then, Ocean Sun." He got to his feet. "It was real good to run into you. I'll send you that map."

He saluted me, and without another word, he turned on his heel and began walking toward the exit. I couldn't believe it. "Constantine!" I blurted, before I could stop myself.

He turned back. He was grinning, of course. I was mortified. I didn't know what to say. I'd lost something, face or footing, by calling to him instead of calling his bluff. I suddenly felt about a hundred years younger than he was, though I didn't even know how old he was. I didn't know anything about him, except his name.

"No one else calls me that," he said.

"I didn't know that," I said, the only thing I could think of to say. "I don't know anything about you."

He cocked his head to the side like an ostrich. He walked backward until he was in front of me again, less than a foot away. "I'm Constantine Brave," he said. "Most people call me Constant and some people call me Brave, but you can call me Constantine. I'm imminently a philosopher. I live with four roommates and about seventeen Geiger counters up in Hamilton Heights. I like to paint, sometimes, where no one else can see. And I'm very pleased to meet you, by the way. I don't know if I've said that yet. And now I've got to run, but I'll catch you again in this life and the next one."

He stuck his hand toward me. It hung there until I remembered I was supposed to shake it. His hand enveloped mine; he shook firmly. My arm bounced like a noodle. He kept grinning until I grinned back.

And then he ran, his windbreaker flapping behind him, his paint canisters ringing like bells long after he was gone. I was dizzy and warm. I realized I was still holding the light slate gray can, for the shuttle that I'd never put on the map. I felt a swift and enormous impulse to jump back onto the tracks and dash once more into the tunnels, just to paint that last line. I hated the feeling of an unfinished thing, like a scab waiting to be picked.

With Constant gone, I once again felt barely substantial, a ghost beneath the city. I stood up. All the blood rushed to my head. My legs had fallen asleep and threatened to give out beneath me. I sat back down.

Constantine, I'd said. I liked the way it had felt on my lips and the way my tongue moved around the syllables; I liked the way it sounded out loud. I hadn't even meant to say it. In my head I'd been thinking of him as Constant the whole time, but it was Constantine that fell out of my mouth.

The train came. It was almost entirely empty, but not quite. I wondered if the people already aboard had been stuck there the whole time, or if they had waited, like I had. I got a good seat, next to a pole against which I could lean my head and close my eyes. First the world had been moving too slowly, and now it was moving too fast.

No one else calls me that, Constant had said. I thought about that the whole way home, clutching the spray paint canister tight against my chest.

STRANGERS AND FRIENDS

In the morning Georgie woke me up so we could bring an order of fake IDs to the Western Union. She did this by making an ungodly amount of noise in the kitchen so that she didn't personally have to rouse me. She'd been traumatized, she'd told me, because everyone in her family was a troll in the morning. Georgie was also a troll. Last week she lobbed a boot at me when I tried to get her up, past noon.

I was already awake, though I hadn't gone to bed until nearly six in the morning. I was combing through my night with Constant, minute by minute, trying to decide how badly I'd mortified myself. Should I be embarrassed to have called him Constantine? Did he think it was lame that I hadn't painted anything, and did he blame me for the map's incompleteness? Did I run weird, and did he notice while he was running behind me? Why, *why* did I tell him I was suicidal? And did any of it really even happen?

The more I thought about it, the more the whole night

seemed like a dream. Sunlight streamed into the apartment. In the full and natural light, the night seemed less real. The sky was back to its normal, friendly blue; when I tried to recall the electric shade from last night, all I could see was this morning's sky. It was like trying to remember a tune while another song played. I had no email from Constant with the promised map.

But then, as we were walking to Western Union, Georgie said, "Did you know the power went out last night?"

We were getting fake IDs because Georgie had recently lost hers to a bouncer in a foul mood. She'd put off acquiring a new one until she'd learned I had never had a fake ID. She was horrified on my behalf, and immediately set off finding seven to twelve more people for the order, to keep down costs. I thought this would take her a few weeks at least, but three days later she'd amassed photos, information, and money from no fewer than fifteen people, which meant we'd only have to fork over seventy-five dollars each. I had done so, reluctantly, after much pressure—another reason I hadn't had enough money for a rideshare last night.

"Yeah," I said. I thought about telling her all that had transpired but didn't know where to begin. To say "I met someone" seemed insufficient.

It didn't matter. Georgie launched into a prolonged explanation of why she and Tashya had left the bar without me. She'd taken several shots backstage with one of the other performers to calm herself down, but she hadn't eaten all day and the shots turned out to be absinthe.

"I've never had absinthe before, I didn't know what I was drinking," said Georgie, as though this explained how one might accidentally ingest five ounces of hundred-proof alcohol. "Then I literally forgot my entire set. Like, I couldn't even remember the joke about that time I peed myself at a bar and didn't know what to do so I bought a pitcher of beer and poured it down the front of my pants, and you know that was so mortifying it's basically branded into my brain. Then I had to puke, because I was so nervous. And Tashya happened to be peeing, so she took me home."

Georgie didn't mention that she and Tashya, hopefully prior to the puking, had kissed so emphatically they'd knocked the cold-water knob clean off the sink. I knew this because the other comedian, perhaps the absinthe supplier, had recounted everything to me in great detail after I'd searched the bar for them. I didn't begrudge Georgie and Tashya, or at least I didn't anymore. It was hard to stay mad at Georgie because she was so tiny. There were other reasons—she was kind and generous and funny and took almost nothing seriously—but mostly it was because Georgie hardly cleared five feet in platform sneakers, the only type of shoe she owned. It was like staying angry at a child.

Georgie insisted on going into Manhattan. When I asked why we couldn't find a closer Western Union, it turned out that she also wanted to go to a very particular store in Soho for a very particular face wash. It never occurred to Georgie that this might be inconvenient for me, because nothing was ever inconvenient for her. Georgie was always running off somewhere to help a friend in need: yesterday to Astoria to help a high school friend build some floating shelves, the day before all the way out to the Rockaways to collect shells with a friend majoring in sculpture. With Georgie, I was always just along for the ride.

I didn't mind much. While Constantine had made me feel like all my circumstances were illusory, Georgie made me feel more grounded. She had such curiosity and affection for life—it was hard to be too gloomy around her.

We walked to the subway. I felt paranoid and kept looking around for the police. I couldn't help but imagine that a security camera had caught my face and Constant's, and we were now among New York's most wanted. Georgie was talking the entire time about a party she wanted to attend, but I was busy running through arrest scenarios until Georgie poked me in the arm and asked me what I was going to wear.

The train pulled into the station. I was overwhelmed. "What?" I said as we got on. "What did you say? Wearing to what?"

There were no seats. We stood by a pole, with a guy wearing earbuds.

"The party," said Georgie. "Arlo said the theme is

communism, but he didn't say if it was pro or anti. So I guess we should just play it safe and wear red. But my red top—you know the one? The off-the-shoulder one—is in my hamper. But not *deep* in my hamper, so I might be able to resuscitate it. I don't know. What if the party is ironically anti-communism and we're the only ones who show up wearing red? What if everyone else is dressed up as McCarthy?"

I could tell the guy with the earbuds had paused his music and was eavesdropping.

"I'm really tired—"

"*No*, Ocean, come on! You have to come. You didn't come to the last one! I promise I'll let you mope in your room for the rest of the week, but you have to come to this. There are people I want you to meet! Please say you'll come. You're coming."

The party was being hosted by one of Georgie's school friends, who (Georgie said) she was much closer to now that she (Georgie) had dropped out. When Georgie was at school, she had sort of hated everyone, except it turned out that she was just sleep-deprived. She hadn't batted an eye when she'd learned I was taking a gap year without a good reason. She was skeptical of higher education to begin with, and besides, she knew plenty of people who took time to find themselves in Nepal or Malawi or, well, New York City.

But I felt like I was squandering time. Most days I was depleted. I felt both dull and absurd. I didn't want to go out and interact with people; even the mention of the party made me feel suddenly wide-awake with panic, like someone was peeling my skin off. All the time I felt guilty, and at least vaguely horrified by what I'd done. My whole life I'd told my mother everything, and now everything I told her was false. But Georgie was always going out, and she always wanted company. Last night I had finally caved, and they'd left me at the bar. But as I watched Georgie chew on her lip, it occurred to me that she was trying to make it up to me. I felt suddenly unkind.

"Well," I relented. "I might leave early."

"That's fine!" Georgie beamed. She had no intention of letting me leave early.

The train trembled on. I asked Georgie if she knew how they built the tunnels under the river, but she only shrugged. I guess this was an effect of having grown up in the city: even the most extraordinary details were mundane. But I thought about the underwater tunnels every time I was on the subway; engineering fell so far outside my reality that it might as well have been magic. So much of life was like this: inconceivable. I couldn't help but feel suspicious that these hidden mechanics were a form of afterlife torture for killing myself—how little I knew, and how no one else seemed to care.

As soon as we got off the train, my phone began to vibrate in my pocket. It was my mother. My hands immediately went clammy; I felt each pore open until the sweat was welling in my palms, a ticklish sensation. It was crazy to me that some of the most extreme things I felt weren't real: my stomach didn't tear its way through my intestines and fall straight to my feet, but it sure felt like it. My heart seemed to swell until it was stuck in my throat, but it wasn't *really* throwing itself against my rib cage like a panicked dog in a crate. I answered the phone.

"Hi, Mama," I said.

"Ocean, how are you?" she said, except this wasn't what she said at all. She said Sun Haiying, my name in Chinese, which was almost Ocean but not quite; and then she said, "How are you like today," or in fact, "Today how are you like." I wasn't sure I believed in translation, as a concept. I wasn't sure you could lay two languages on top of each other and pretend like they matched.

In Chinese, my name means something close to "shadow that passes over the ocean." My grandfather had named me. He had been on his deathbed, so everyone had to defer to him, though he had picked a dreadful name. My grandmother had even consulted a woman who calculated fortunes, who agreed it was inauspicious. My grandpa named me this because my mother was leaving for America—because he would never meet me, because he could not imagine me except as a shadow over the sea, the wing of a bird with nowhere to land. Every time I thought about this, my nose smarted like I might cry.

"I'm okay," I said, then, "I'm a little tired."

"You have to sleep more," she said severely, and launched into a story about the son of someone she knew from church, who'd contracted stomach ulcers after studying so hard he only slept for two hours a night.

"I'll sleep more," I said.

"Good," she said. She was on her lunch break and she hoped I was on mine too. She was glad to have caught me between classes. Or was I done with classes for the day?

Then I was sweating all over. Sometimes when my mother called I could get by without lying outright, mumbling responses and answering sideways until she had to go. It was lucky (for me) that my mother was a middle manager at an insurance company, because she worked long hours and I could always count on some crisis to call her away. But now I was in a bind: yes was a lie, but no was too.

But she steamrolled on. "I saw on the news that New York City lost power last night." My mother spoke in statements. I saw, I did, I heard. She was so sure of herself. You would never guess this by looking at her. My mother, like me, was superficially unremarkable: not short and not tall, not diminutive but also not intimidating, and lately, I had noticed, getting older. In my mind's eye she still looked the way she did when I was four or five: thirty and lovely, with long dark hair. When I looked at her now, the memory laid on top of reality like film on water, and time felt dissonant.

"Yeah," I said. "But I slept through the whole thing."

Georgie and I kept shouldering our way through the station. I turned away from her, a little, when I said that. My tongue was fat and guilty. But I'd said exactly what my mother wanted to hear. She told me to stay safe and eat well, and to study hard but not so hard that I got stomach ulcers. Then she had to go.

"I love you," she said, and my throat closed so fiercely that I looked around to check that no one around me was eating a kiwi, to which I am allergic.

"I love you too," I garbled out, but she'd already ended the call.

Outside, the day was wickedly hot, and the back of my neck broke out into a furious sweat. I pocketed my phone. The street was absurdly crowded. Great throngs of people bumped against each other, glared and elbowed, trudged stubbornly on. The sun was the angriest of all, garish with heat.

"Did you really get home before the power went out?" Georgie asked. She worked hard to keep her voice neutral, but I could tell she was asking to absolve herself.

"Yeah," I said. Then, also, "I just didn't want my mother to worry."

Lies and lies. The truth, strangest of all: the blue light, the subway tunnels, Constant with his pockets full of paint. Last night felt like a dream, but I sort of liked that. By not talking about it, I was preserving some essential, surreal part of it. Talking about it would only ruin it.

At the Western Union we stood in line behind a family of Italian tourists trying to exchange a fat belt bag of euros. The father, sweating profusely in the unventilated space, was gesticulating too wildly for the small vestibule, trying to explain to the teller that the prices in Little Italy were just absurd. "Eighteen dollars for mozzarella!" he was shouting. "This country is mad."

"Sir, how much would you like to exchange today?" said the teller dully, like this was not her first time asking the question.

Georgie tapped him on the shoulder. "The Little Italy in the Bronx has better prices, if you don't mind the trek," she said, "and their mozzarella is better. Also, the exchange rate here is terrible. There's a place in Chinatown with a much better rate for euros—do you have a pen? I'll give you the address."

The Italian family had no pens, only cash. I dug through my pockets and produced a stubby pencil. Georgie scribbled an address on Eldridge Street on the back of a money-order envelope and hurried them out the door. The teller scowled at us.

"Hi," Georgie said, scooting to the counter, oblivious. "We're wiring some money to Shenzhen."

Georgie handled the transaction. The teller did everything at a snail's pace, glaring at Georgie every chance she got. I had a strong feeling that I had just lost seventy-five dollars.

Georgie's face wash cost forty dollars before tax. The store was one of the strangest places I'd ever been. It was very *slightly* many things: the walls were slightly curved, and along them the great mirrors were slightly warped, and everything was slightly pink, down to the slightly oversized denim jumpsuits on all the ethnically ambiguous employees. Georgie checked out on an iPad and received a package via a conveyor belt: everything was slightly futuristic, slightly bizarre, seriously trendy, like Anna Wintour had opened a chocolate factory. I was relieved when we left.

On the train, I checked my email again. There was still nothing from Constant. I was surprised by how my stomach twisted. Surely he was awake by now. The longer my inbox remained empty, the more I was convinced that the night before had never happened—that I'd fallen asleep in the station and dreamed it all, or that I'd actually killed myself last summer and everything since was an illusion.

But whenever my mind wandered, it settled on his face. I could recall it perfectly. Faces from my dreams blurred within minutes of my waking and then disappeared forever, but Constant's face remained like it had always been there.

Constantine, I thought, again and again. *Constant.*

"What did you say?" Georgie said.

"Nothing," I said quickly.

She arched an eyebrow. Georgie had extremely versatile eyebrows that were capable of conveying a great range of emotion, and right now, without saying a word, her eyebrow called me a liar. But she let it go. "So, Tashya's busy until late, so she's going to meet us at the party. I guess it'll be like, what, four-ish, by the time we get home. So we have time to do a face mask and I'll do my makeup and then I'll do yours. And we have to rescue my red shirt." Georgie didn't stop talking the whole way home.

After the train it was the deli for sandwiches and juice, the bank for cash, the liquor store where Georgie wove a long story for the cashier about how she'd left her ID at the bar the night before but had had an affair with the bartender on duty today and thus could not retrieve it until tomorrow. In the end the cashier sold us the bottle just to shut her up. When Georgie caught me staring at her, she lifted her chin and said, "Do you have any idea how hard it is to sneak alcohol when you have two dads? I can get away with anything."

Georgie's parents live on the Upper West Side, with a view of Central Park and a full roof terrace. Before I met Georgie, I thought wealth was something totally different. I thought it was brick houses in the nice part of town and spring break in Florida, and a job at an office instead of a factory or nail salon. But here wealth meant millions and billions. One of Georgie's dads had a corporate law practice and the other was some sort of big neurosurgeon at Presbyterian. To Georgie, forty bucks was probably just what face wash cost.

Back at the apartment, Georgie poured shots. Before I came to New York I'd never had anything stronger than beer, and then only once or twice. But my first weekend here Georgie and Tashya had gotten me so drunk I remembered very little of what had happened at all, and then in the morning I had my first hangover and puked in the shower onto my bare feet. But now Georgie handed me a shot and wouldn't let me hand it back, so I took it, and then chugged heavily on the juice Georgie had bought.

"I tried to collect shot glasses," Georgie said, examining her own shot glass, which was emblazoned with CEBU and several mangos, "one from every airport I traveled through. But then I never wanted to use them, because whenever I brought them out, someone broke one. So now I just buy alcohol from duty-free."

I couldn't imagine being friends with Georgie at any other time of my life. It seemed distinctly impossible that she would have paid me any attention had we not ended up in an apartment together. She made me take a second shot. I tossed it in my mouth and nearly puked. Georgie handed me the juice and I drank it, miserably.

Georgie dressed me in a red tank top and a pair of jeans

so full of holes I was worried they'd fall apart while I was wearing them. She dug her own red shirt out of her hamper and doused it in perfume, and then we walked to the party. It wasn't far. The heat had abated, and the evening was beautiful. Georgie started in on the host of the party—some sort of psychopath but the sort Georgie liked—as we walked.

I couldn't stop thinking about Constant. What if he was some sort of psychopath? I wasn't sure there was a sort *I* liked, but I thought I liked him, or at least I liked the time we'd spent together. Had we really painted a subway tunnel last night? What if he never emailed? What if I never saw him again? I tried to wrap my head around that: that he could appear and then disappear, that this was what people did. They came into your life and stayed for some random period of time, and then they left, quickly or quietly or painfully. Maybe he didn't want to email me. Maybe I bored him. By the time I had that thought, we had arrived.

THE TRAIN OF THESEUS

The party was on the roof. We could hear it from the street: the thrumming bass line from the speakers high above, bouncing off all the surrounding buildings as we waited to be buzzed in. I felt like we were in a music box, tiny and enclosed. Finally, several minutes later, the door opened and we climbed six flights of stairs and out a rickety door, to the most spectacular sunset I'd ever seen in my life. Even Georgie, in the middle of a sentence, fell quiet as we stepped out onto the roof. The clouds were vividly pink, and so close I was stunned. Toward the horizon they grew violet, blue, gold. I felt a sudden visceral urge to tell Georgie about last night's sky, to describe it to someone before I forgot it. Already I was uncertain of my memory.

Before I could say anything, Georgie squealed. "Tashya!"

She sprinted across the roof and into Tashya's arms. A full head taller, Tashya gave me a wave around Georgie's wild hair. Then she looked down at Georgie. Her face was both abashed and delighted; I felt almost embarrassed to see her expression, an intimate thing. Tashya was one of the prettiest people I'd ever seen in real life, with dark hair that fell past her waist and a perfectly symmetrical face. It was hard not to think of her prettiness as an essential part of her, like it was her contribution to the world. I felt really depressed every time I thought this.

I didn't want to stand there with them, not knowing what to do with my hands. There were probably thirty other people on the roof, none of whom I knew. No one was dressed as a communist, except for one guy with a Trotsky blowout that could have been a regular blowout. Everyone was crowded by a big trash can that turned out to be filled with alcohol. Beside it was a nightstand stacked precariously with mugs, along with a sign that said NO PONG WITH ANY OF THE HANDMADE CERAMICS. NO SINGLE-USE PLASTIC IN OUR HOME. Since all the mugs were ceramic and looked handmade, no one was playing pong, but they dipped their cups into the trash can and pulled them out brimming with a violent blue liquid. I wasn't sure about drinking out of the garbage, or about having another drink at all. It was too much to navigate.

I went to sit at the edge of the roof. There was a flimsy railing around the perimeter, but I could sit at the fire escape and dangle my legs over six floors of empty space and think about Constant. I was thrilled by the height; it felt fitting to think about him as I sat like this, with my chest full of cold air, though the night was mild and warm.

I'd never told anyone about my inclination to jump off tall things, except him. It wasn't exactly a conversational topic that came up. Sitting now at the edge of the roof, oscillating between wanting to hold tight to the railing and wanting to launch myself off the edge, I felt both relieved and mortified that he knew this particular detail about me. I kept thinking about what he'd said, how even a meaningless life was better than nothing, and being stuck in a terrible place was better than not being. In the tunnel last night, maybe he had been telling me that he knew how I felt—that he knew what it was like to want to close your eyes for longer than a single night's sleep. But the more I ran that moment through my head, the easier it was to convince myself I'd misunderstood him, and the more humiliated I became. Who would email after that? I was miserable.

Someone sat down next to me. It was Tashya.

"Hey," she said. "Look, sorry about last night."

I didn't know how to respond. I didn't want her to be sorry, exactly. I wanted us all to move on.

"It's really okay," I assured her, and then before she could launch into a whole speech, I said, "How was class?"

Tashya was older than Georgie or me. She was so old that I was terrified of her when we first met: twenty-one, astronomical. She was a junior at one of the best conservatories in the world, and at the end of each day she was haggard with exhaustion. She told me she once sat in a practice room for eighteen hours straight without noticing any time had passed. I told her this was a form of torture, like solitary confinement.

My second night in the apartment, she came home in a rage because she'd been kicked out of her practice room after running the same measure in a Ravel piece one thousand two hundred and sixty-six times consecutively. She wasn't furious that she'd been kicked out, but that after a thousand times she still wasn't touching a particular note correctly. Georgie and I had been baffled. "I'm just not touching it *right*," she kept saying, "the quality just isn't *right*." There was no way to comfort her. She'd disappeared into her room and was gone again before either of us woke up the next day. Tashya was the best pianist in Slovenia—she had played her first concerto with a full orchestra when she was seven years old. But at the conservatory, everyone was best: the best violinist in Luxembourg, the best flutist in Spain, the best operatic soprano in Taiwan. She had a particular feud with a guy who was supposedly the best pianist in all of California and had thus been spending nearly all her time between classes lying in wait for a free piano.

"Horrible," said Tashya, glum. "I hate Philosophy of Music. I can't stand sitting in that classroom while Thomas Sato drops names of philosophers that *I know* he's never read.

Anyone who says they've read Kant is lying. I hate philosophy on principle, of course. Music is just sine and cosine, Ocean, it's just variations on the sound wave, and the fact that it makes us feel sublime things is purely incidental. I don't believe in the work of *making meaning*. Some people like Mozart and some people detest him. If there's meaning in chance, I don't care about it. I'm going to skip class on Thursday and go straight to a practice room. God knows Thomas Sato would never ditch the chance to listen to himself talk for an hour, so hopefully one will be open."

"Isn't talking about music sort of like music?" I asked. I thought so, which was the trouble with language. How could you talk to anyone if none of the words you knew were the right ones? What if you couldn't even make the right sounds? I wanted to tell Tashya about Constant more than I had wanted to tell Georgie, because Georgie would only become sentimental and romantic, but Tashya was more likely to frown me back to reason.

Tashya swatted the air with her hand. "This is a semantic argument, Ocean. I won't hear it. If you stretch the meaning of the word *music* to include language or conversation, then—sure. But you see that this is just the problem, this . . . making of meaning."

I saw she was right. This made me feel worse about Constant. Maybe nothing had happened between us at all. Maybe we had been talking about different things; maybe we had felt opposite feelings, and this was why he wasn't ever going to email me.

"Anyway," said Tashya, "I *am* sorry about last night. Georgie really was just wildly inebriated. I've never seen her so incoherent. She vomited into a fedora we found on the platform. I heard you made it back before the power went out, though."

I was distressed. It was a tiny lie told for the greater good, but all the same it made me feel awful to see it spread. "Yeah," I said.

"She's not hungover at all," observed Tashya. We turned to squint at Georgie filling (or refilling) a mug with trash punch. She laughed at something someone said to her, then chugged with great verve. Tashya shook her head. "Unbelievable. She's got the drinking tolerance of a failed Russian poet in the body of a small child. Just a marvel. An absolute freak of nature."

If I had felt left out when they ditched me at the bar last night, I felt ten times more so now. I had been the last to move into our apartment. By the time I got there, Tashya and Georgie were already flirting. At first they were funny and interesting to watch. Georgie was smitten. The first week I lived there she couldn't look Tashya in the eye without dissolving into silliness. And Tashya was even worse. She developed a tic of clearing her throat after every third word whenever she talked to Georgie.

But when their conversational spasms finally cleared, it was like they had fallen into a language of their own. When the three of us were together, I was outside their jokes and affections; it always felt a little like I was eavesdropping on something I didn't understand. Which was okay, except for the mornings when I heard them eating breakfast together outside my closed door, or when I caught Georgie grinning at Tashya when she thought no one else was looking, or when they accidentally made eye contact and out of nowhere became incredibly, silently shy. When this happened, I felt like the loneliest person in the world.

I tried to imagine someone looking at me the way Tashya was looking at Georgie.

"I'm going to get a drink," Tashya finally said, and beelined for Georgie. When I looked over my shoulder a few minutes later, they were already dancing. The light cast them in pink and gold, and something welled in me painfully, like tears.

Despite myself, I checked my email again. There was a new message. I was so surprised I almost dropped my phone off the roof. There was his name in my inbox: Constantine Brave, like I had conjured it. Relief rushed through me so fast I felt weak at my joints—the night had happened after all, and neither Constant nor I was an apparition.

Then I was confused. It was not an email at all but an invitation to a cloud document. When I clicked through, my stomach went sour with disappointment: it was just a map.

It was better than nothing, I told myself. I didn't feel like I was losing my mind anymore, wondering if I was capable of conjuring up a whole person, a whole night. And it really was a spectacular map. When I'd first arrived in the city I'd cried in front of the subway map at Barclays Center, trying to untangle the mass of colorful lines. Constant's map showed all the train lines and all their stops, labeled cleanly in tiny black letters. It showed all the places where you could transfer trains and even some places where you could transfer to a bus. I traced the screen of my phone with my fingernail, imagining Constant painting it with the same sure strokes he'd painted with last night: the arc of his arm, the shape of his back in the dark.

I kept scrolling down the map, and only then did I notice there was a second page. I held my phone so tightly my knuckles went white.

He wrote:

Last night after I left you, I dreamed I was Theseus leaving the labyrinth. (Well, in fact immediately after I left you, I walked to a different station and took a different train; I suppose this makes you the Ariadne I left behind for the wine god. It was Diana Wynne Jones, wasn't it, who said this meant she fell to drinking? I toast you if you did.) At the other station my train came almost immediately, if you can believe it, but in my dream it did not. In this dream in which I was Theseus, I sat on a bench for ages, eons. And finally a C train came. It was very late, you remember, so there were no express trains. On the C line runs the oldest trains in the city: the R32 model, the Brightliners, first introduced in 1964. They're an absolute relic, but just imagine them unveiled almost six decades ago, and how impressive they must have seemed among the rest of the fleet, which still had wicker seats. Trains of the future, they said! And in my dream I thought, *Damn, they were right, here I am in the future, still on these trains.* But as soon as I stood up to board the train, the doors opened and I heard the conductor say, "This train is being held at the station by the dispatcher." Out rushed hundreds of MTA employees in their neon vests and immediately they began to tear the train apart. I couldn't believe my eyes. I had been waiting for hours, days. Right in front of me they were dismantling this perfectly fine train: unscrewing the doors, replacing the windowpanes, then the seats, then even the shell, even the links between train cars holding it all together. I blinked, and when I opened my eyes again the train was a whole different model, one I had never seen before, with bright yellow seats and open gangways. The neon vests disappeared as quickly as they'd come, and the doors opened again. I heard the conductor say, "Due to construction, this train is now running on the B line." So in the dream I walked home. I woke up still trying to figure out when, exactly, the train had ceased to be a C train.

Of course, it was all a dream. In real life the MTA employees would only get halfway through disassembling the car before construction stalled because the transit president had quit, or the unions failed to reach an agreement with the construction executives, or the city ran out of money. You can fix a map, but a map can't fix a system.

That was all he had written. I read it five times while swinging my legs off the fire escape. The last of the sunset turned blue, then indigo, and then the New York dark I had come to expect: an inky violet webbed with the day's pollution, and the brightest moonlight I'd ever seen anywhere in my life. Below, the ground became infinite in the dark, but I had never wanted to jump less. When Georgie came to haul me to my feet to go dance with her and Tashya, I only resisted a little bit.

UNTITLED DOCUMENT

Several days passed before I could write to Constant. The longer I waited, the more impossible it became to say anything at all. I wanted to thank him for the map, and respond to his dream. I tried to dream something clever and funny to describe to him, but I became so anxious trying to dream that I barely slept at all. Then I was so tired I slept through most of the next day. When I woke up it was early afternoon. I read his message thirteen more times, until I had most of it memorized. I read the line about me—the bit about Ariadne—so many times my eyes blurred. At first I was flattered, and it made my chest feel fluttery. But the more I read it, the less convinced I was that it was a compliment. It was accessory to the rest of the message, the way Ariadne was accessory to Theseus. I got caught up on the words *left behind* and read them again and again. What did that mean, left behind? Could it mean that he didn't want me to respond at all—that his note was just an accompaniment to the map I had asked for?

You can fix a map, but a map can't fix a system. This sounded final, like it was the proper conclusion to draw from his dream. But I thought he was saying something else entirely. I thought the dream, like most dreams, was about losing yourself. It was about sitting still for so long you began to dissolve: face, self, memory, pulling pith from flesh, until you lost something essential. I felt unreasonably upset that we seemed to disagree on this.

I slept for fourteen hours. I woke again in a fit of panic—like I had missed some deadline to respond, and every minute made it worse. I opened the document and stared at the blinking cursor and couldn't think of a single thing to say. I closed the document.

I was running out of money. Nothing was cheap. Utilities were expensive and the train was expensive and food was astronomical. During the summers before I moved to New York, I had worked at a bookstore in the mall, a job at which I was thoroughly incompetent. Every summer I had to learn the alphabet again, and when I shelved new arrivals I had to sing the whole sequence under my breath. Despite all this I had saved up nearly eight thousand dollars, which I had hoped to stretch for five or six months—or at least until I could find a job here. But after only a month, half of it had disappeared. I had no idea how much money it took to stay alive. It had cost several grand just to move into an apartment, and train fare was at least a hundred every month, and even a coffee could soar into the double digits.

My card was declined again when Georgie and I went to get bagels. Georgie didn't think it was a big deal; she paid for my bagel and started talking about Tashya. But I was close to a panic attack. At the rate I was spending, I only had a month or so left until my bank account was completely empty. What was I going to do if I couldn't pay rent next month? I'd have to ask my mother for help, and explain how I was not at college but bumming around in Brooklyn, that I had wasted all of my own money and was locked in a lease I couldn't afford.

"You're not eating," Georgie observed. She herself was barely a quarter of the way through her bagel. Between every bite she used the side of her pinky to sweep up the sesame and poppy seeds that fell off her bagel and sprinkle them back on top of her lox. It was time-consuming work, especially because her head was buried in her phone. "Anyway, do you think Tashya liked my friends the other night? She seemed grumpy, didn't she? I know it was kind of a weird group."

Before she dropped out to be a comedian, Georgie had gone to art school, and her art school friends were as colorful as she was. All the girls had enormous eyes and nose piercings, and all of the boys wore tiny beanies with their ears sticking out. Georgie had introduced me to people with names like Iggy and Willoughby and Seb. The theme had indeed been communism, and by the end of the night we were talking about the means of production, and Iggy had offered to lend me his copy of *Das Kapital*.

Georgie slammed her phone on the table, sending poppy seeds flying. "She just literally *never* texts me back. Do you think she's ignoring me? Why would she ignore me? I'm hilarious."

I was wary. "Isn't she in class?"

"So?" demanded Georgie.

I wasn't sure what else to say. It was true that Tashya was atrocious at texting. Two days before, I'd texted her asking if I could borrow some toothpaste, and this morning she had texted back to say help myself.

"*Hmmm,*" said Georgie, and then, "You've been out of it, too."

Her jaw was set in a way that meant I couldn't just shrug off the comment. Georgie was in a combative mood, waspish and itching for a fight. Georgie was at her worst when left alone with her thoughts: she was always on her phone, switching between apps, texting ten people at once. I watched her pinch up more seeds from her bagel and redistribute them on top. I didn't want to tell her I was worried about money, because saying out loud made it more real, and more dire.

"I'm just tired," I said.

"You sleep more than anyone I know," Georgie said, though she herself probably slept as much as I did. Then suddenly she brightened. This was something I liked about Georgie, except when I didn't: her moods were like the weather in the upper Midwest, where you had to dress for snow and summer on the same day. "Oh, before I forget—my parents invited us for dinner tomorrow night. They're excited that I finally have friends without food restrictions. They can't believe *both* you and Tashya eat meat *and* lactose *and* gluten *and* nuts."

In fact I was lactose intolerant, but it was already too late to mention it. I was relieved to not have to pay for dinner. I had been skipping meals to save money, and my pants were starting to get loose. I definitely didn't have money for new pants.

That night I opened Constant's document again. Two things had changed. Until now, the document had no name and was labeled UNTITLED DOCUMENT in small gray letters in one corner. Now it said UNTITLED DOCUMENT in bold— Constant had changed it. I didn't know what he meant by it. Did he want me to come up with a title? Did he want the document to be called UNTITLED DOCUMENT?

And he had added something. After his paragraph, set apart to call attention to itself, he had written:

I was wondering about your name.

I felt like I had swallowed a lungful of helium. I stood up and sat back down, and stood up again. I held my hands out to check if they were shaking; they weren't, though I felt full of ants, or like I had been shot through with electricity. I kept jumping to my feet. I checked the editing history in the document. Constant had made one change at 12:39 p.m., and another at 12:43 p.m. I marveled at the time stamps. We had just missed each other. I had been reading his messages at the bagel shop ten minutes before that.

I could write about my name, I thought. I started typing, before I could change my mind.

No one could pronounce my Chinese name on the attendance sheet, and so one of three things must have happened: my mother translated my name to English—Ocean—in consideration of my teachers, or my teachers asked what my name meant and changed it in consideration to themselves, or I translated it personally, to make my own life easier. This last one is the most likely, I think, since Ocean is actually an abysmal translation.

I have this idea that I am two different people under these two different names. Names matter, I think: the bouba/kiki effect shows us the naming of objects is not completely arbitrary. The funny thing is, my name in English is the opposite of my name in Chinese. In one language my name means shadow on the ocean, and in the other my name is Ocean Sun. Probably Ocean Sun and Sun Haiying are two different people, and people would have treated them differently. No one wants to talk to you if they are shy about saying your name out loud. Ocean, it seems, at least prompts people to wonder.

There must have been a time I answered to both, and then a tipping point, when I started thinking of myself more as Ocean and less as Sun Haiying. I thought this was what your dream was about—the way you are always losing yourself. Shedding skin cells and recollection like bread crumbs in a forest, only to turn around to find that they've disappeared, and you are lost in the dark.

It was at once too intimate and too scattered; I had said both too much and too little. I wanted to delete it, but it wouldn't have mattered. Constant could go into the edit history and see what the document looked like at any given moment, could see every letter I had typed or deleted, could follow my cursor back and forth across his screen just as it had moved across mine.

I printed out thirty copies of my résumé and walked around Manhattan trying to drop them off. Literally no one wanted one. I went to several coffee shops and got flatly dismissed because I had no experience. The restaurants said the same thing. One place, apparently, was quite famous, and the hostess laughed in my face. "Do you know how many people want to work here?" I didn't.

By noon I was drenched in sweat. It poured off my nose and temples. Seeing me in such a state, people wanted my résumé even less. I happened across a used bookstore, where an employee around my age wrinkled her nose as she looked down at my slightly damp résumé. "We don't have any open positions," she told me, "but we only take online applications anyway." The bookseller and I stared at each other, not knowing what to say. In the end I bought a copy of *The*

Little Prince, which was on display at the counter, just to have something to do with my hands. It cost two or three times more than I expected it to, and then I descended into an atrocious mood at having spent so much money.

The heat quickly became unbearable. I went to see Tashya. By the time I walked to the conservatory, I was light-headed and seeing purple hues in the haze, like the world had been dipped in dye. Tashya was alarmed when she came to retrieve me from the sidewalk. Inside, the air-conditioning was so strong it made me dizzy, and I broke out head to toe in goose bumps. I had to sit on a long bench in the lobby for several minutes before I could climb the two flights of stairs to the practice room Tashya had claimed for the day.

She was trying to relearn a fingering pattern on a Ravel concerto and told me to occupy myself for another hour. I opened *The Little Prince*. It was the first book I had ever read in English, and I had adored it so much that I'd read my secondhand copy to tatters and never bought another, until now. I couldn't believe how little I really remembered. My impression of the book had faded to colors and caricatures: the surly rose, the Sahara desert, the little planet where the sun rose and set all day. I had forgotten all the funny adults on their dismal planets. The lamplighter, in particular, seemed to speak to me intimately. He too behaved like someone whose life was constantly on the brink of disaster.

Eventually I picked up my phone. Tashya was playing

the same seven or eight notes again and again. Once every twenty iterations she said something vulgar in Slovenian and started again. I checked the UNTITLED DOCUMENT. I didn't expect anything new; Constant would probably take two or three or four days to respond, if ever. But when I scrolled down past the map, a great chunk of text was missing, most of it mine.

I panicked. Had I deleted it accidentally? I went into the edit history. At 3 p.m., an hour earlier, Constant had logged into the document, highlighted the whole thing, and deleted it. My blood rushed to my head and I felt my cheeks go bright red. Why would Constant delete what I had written?

I read what remained.

Another time I will tell you about my name

It was a different paragraph. He'd deleted everything we had written and started again. I scanned the rest of the history: there, recovered, were his paragraphs about Theseus, and mine about names. I was relieved, then embarrassed by how relieved I felt. The near-blank document had made me feel full of loss, but now that I stared at it, recovered, I felt childish.

I thought again of Theseus and his train. I wondered if Constant was making a point. He wrote:

Another time I will tell you about my name, because it is not an interesting story. I think you're right that translation is a little like the train scenario: you replace this piece and that piece and at the end you say, Look, nothing has changed. But of course everything has changed. For this reason I don't believe much in the value of translation.

I took a sharp breath; it seemed to jab me between the ribs. I wondered if he had read what I had written, and if he had, why he would say my name and my selfhood weren't valuable.

I've been thinking more about the afterlife. I've read about people who have had a near-death experience, wherein they experience physical death—their heart stops, brain activity ceases—and yet, when they are resuscitated, they report remarkable experiences, and insist their consciousness continued even though they showed all the signs of biological death.

Sisyphus is perhaps our best example of the near-death experience. In fact he cheated death twice. First he betrayed the river nymph Aegina, who was hiding from her father. When the god of death, Thanatos, tried to punish him by chaining him in hell, Sisyphus managed to chain Thanatos instead. Then no one living could die, and the old and the sick suffered. The gods came together to force Sisyphus back to hell. But before he died again, he told his wife to trash his body, so in the Underworld he could plead with their bureaucrats: "Look how this woman has maligned me! At least allow me to leave the Underworld for a proper burial." Accordingly they let him out, and the gods had to be dispatched *again* to drag him off, and to trap him behind the Styx with a large boulder and a steep hill.

Say, when you die, or get very close to dying, you fall into a lengthy dream—lengthy because you lose your physical relationship to time and space. You dream and dream. Is this the same thing as afterlife? I think so. Any difference is semantic. Sisyphus had the worst dream of all, but was the monotony so much worse than life? Now I understand why you were so baffled to see me in the train station, undead. When we are dreaming, we think we are awake. We rely on our senses to distinguish reality from simulation, but clearly they are not always up to the task; we could be dead right now, both of us, dead and dreaming. And so when you asked me if I was dead, you were really asking if we shared the same delusion, to which I say: yes.

"Ocean. *Ocean.*"

I blinked. I looked up. Tashya had turned around on the piano bench. I felt warm from my toes all the way to my hairline. *You were really asking if we shared the same delusion, to which I say: yes.* The line played in my head like a prayer circle; I was light-headed and dizzy, and couldn't seem to stop smiling. Tashya saw the book beside me and wrinkled her nose.

"Is that *Le Petit Prince?*"

Tashya had read the book in the original French, and hated it. Because she was Slovene, Tashya spoke Slovenian, French, German, and English fluently, Spanish and Italian and Russian passably, and Hungarian and Czech rudimentarily. When she liked a book, she always read it in more than one language. She had barely read *The Little Prince* once.

"It's sort of a—what's the word? Fraternité book, no?"

"What do you mean?"

She shrugged. There was a little frown scrunching her nose. "Boys teaching boys philosophical things, marveling at their own wit. The only female character is a self-obsessed rose, who, you know, was based on Saint-Exupéry's estranged Salvadoran wife. It dismally fails the Bechdel test and exoticizes *and* objectifies. Let them all die in the desert, I say."

It was hard to argue with her. Tashya was sure of herself, though in a different way than Georgie. Georgie held her opinion before her like a gun, paving the way. Tashya just had fewer qualms about subjectivity of experience: she thought of truth as a precise, mathematical thing. She had an idea of things and she stood up for it; she had an opinion. Tashya said this was the reason she was able to do so well in America, and I agreed. I was sure it was also the reason I seemed to do so badly in America, or anywhere. I thought opinions were difficult. I was baffled that everyone else seemed to have so many—how they preferred their coffee and which politician was the stupidest, what was wrong or right or pointless in the world. I felt like I didn't know enough about anything to have an opinion.

Tashya showed me around the conservatory. Down a long hall, I heard the strains of an orchestra starting and stopping, interrupted time and time again by an impatient voice and a wayward bassoon. There were two floors of practice rooms, and every single one was occupied. Tashya pointed out a corner room. "Thomas Sato is in there," she said. "That's the best piano room in the school, except for the ones upstairs for the grad students. It has a huge window that looks over Lincoln Center and the only baby grand. Somehow Thomas Sato gets it almost every single day. Once I made it up here at seven in the morning and he was already in there running scales." She sighed. "I've literally only practiced there twice, in all three years I've been here. I wish him carpal tunnel."

We ended up in the nosebleeds of the concert hall, where it was dim and quiet and smelled pleasantly of wood. On the stage was a full concert grand, nine feet long, though from where we sat it looked as small as a toy. Tashya told me that one day when she was rich, she was going to buy an unbleached Bösendorfer Imperial. "The Bösendorfer Imperial has ninety-seven keys, a full eight octaves. That's ten notes more than a regular piano. The extra notes are all on the bass end, and all of them are black. I wonder what they sound like. I can't imagine it; it's like imagining colors at the beginning of the rainbow, before red. I know they must exist. But I can't imagine it."

I admired her, her head lolling back against the seat, the closest I'd seen her to slouching in the whole time I'd known her. I thought of Tashya's face as something that protected her, unlike mine, which revealed me, and made me vulnerable.

"Kim Kardashian has an unbleached Steinway," she said. "But better her than Thomas Sato."

We were quiet for so long I thought Tashya had fallen asleep, or I had. It was impossible to tell how much time had passed. There were no windows in the concert hall, and all sound was muted. I was itching for my phone, to check the UNTITLED DOCUMENT, to reread what Constant had written. I was worried I was developing a compulsive habit—I couldn't seem to set my phone down for more than five or ten minutes. But every time I thought about his last line, *You were really asking me if we shared the same delusion, to which I say: yes,* I felt a thrill go through me.

When I reread it, though, I wasn't sure that Constantine's response was encouraging. Why was he so concerned with Sisyphus? Was he confirming that I was dead or refuting it? Was the delusion we shared life or hell? What did mythology have to do with my anxiety that it was too late, that I had already killed myself and ended up in this strange limbo where all my circumstances were so expensive and so punitive?

When Tashya spoke it seemed unnaturally loud, and startled me.

"Do you think Georgie thinks I'm . . . I don't know." She paused for so long I wasn't sure it was going to be a conversation. "Did Georgie say anything about me at all?"

I glanced at her. "Well," I said, "she said she was trying to text you."

Tashya stared determinedly at her hands. Then she let out a sharp breath. "The thing is," she said, "I don't really have service in the practice rooms. Doesn't she know that? Her other friends, from the party. What did you think?"

I thought they were wild, in a Sendak way, like we had passed a bend in the river and found them dancing with their arms in the sky. I didn't think this was exactly what Tashya was asking me.

"Do you think they're all texting each other?" she asked. "All day long, every day?"

It seemed to take a great effort for Tash to ask. I admired the crease between her eyebrows, and then I was ashamed. I said, "I can't imagine that they're texting *all* day."

"I can't either," she said, "but yesterday she sent me sixty-nine texts. Did she do that on purpose? I just—" She took another sharp breath, like someone was punching her in the chest. "What is there to say over text? Why can't we wait to say it face-to-face? Shouldn't we want *more* context with communication, not less?"

Then it was my turn to feel punched in the chest. I itched for my phone, to read what Constant had written. On one hand I agreed with Tashya—but I also thought of communication as something that happened *despite* context, not because of it, and maybe that was why I liked the untitled document. Our conversations had almost no context at all. They seemed to float in space, suspended.

"Communication is impossible," I agreed.

"And now she's angry," sighed Tashya. "Ocean, I wish someone had read me *Much Ado About Nothing* instead of fairy tales when I was little. No one tells you love is mostly miscommunication. Or that life is. I don't know what to do."

I had a horrible vision of sharing an apartment with Georgie and Tashya while they fell out of love with each other: Georgie, who was prone to shouting, and Tashya, who would avoid the apartment more and more until she was sleeping at the conservatory, finally disappearing from our lives altogether. "Are you two breaking up?" I asked, dreading the answer.

"I don't even think we're together," she said. "Are we? We've never talked about it. Yesterday Georgie sent me a meme about commitment issues. But why? Why can't we just say what we mean?"

If only things were so simple, I thought.

Tashya allowed herself to mope for another moment, and then drew herself up severely. "I know it's silly," she said. "I know everything is fine. I don't know why we never talk about anything serious. We kiss, and we make each other laugh, and everything feels fine, like hammering out the details is extraneous, and only what we feel is real. Then we leave each other, and nothing in the world feels right."

I felt a rush of tenderness for her. When I first met her, I thought that being Tashya must feel entirely different than being me. Even now, she looked only beautiful and severe, her long thick hair falling in soft waves down her stern spine. Georgie was so different. Her eyes were always full of emotion, and her desire to be loved was plain on her face. I could see where their tension came from, but I couldn't explain it to either of them; I couldn't put it in words. Georgie felt things as deeply as I did, but Tashya would always tell me the truth.

"Do you think her parents will like me?" Tashya said, after a long time.

"Of course they will."

"How can you know?"

I was almost overwhelmed by my desire to reach out and hold her hand. Her sharp angles had melted, and she looked so forlorn I didn't know what else to do. My hand twitched; then I felt shy. I didn't reach for her.

"Oh, Tash," I said. "How could they not?"

Georgie met us in the station. She was dressed more conservatively than I'd ever seen her, in plain jeans and a floral blouse. She kept fidgeting with her collar.

"My dads don't know about my tattoos," Georgie explained to me, before she turned to Tashya and they began to bicker. Georgie couldn't believe Tashya had ignored Georgie all day.

Tashya reminded her that she didn't have service at the conservatory. Georgie thought this was an awfully convenient excuse. Tashya said it was just a consistent one—she *never* had service at the conservatory. I fell a few steps behind them. Even when they were fighting, they had no time for anything but each other.

The townhouse was only two blocks from the subway, on a quiet street that was completely unlike Brooklyn, even the nicer parts. The townhouses here were taller, somehow European, old and imperial. I fought the urge to dig at my ears. We stopped before a house that looked like all the others, but as we climbed the shale steps it seemed to grow taller, and wider, which is to say I felt smaller and smaller.

Both of Georgie's dads opened the door. Behind them stood a very small dog and an extremely large dog. The dogs were equally delighted to see Georgie, but while the small one could only paw at her ankles, the large one rose on its hind legs and towered over her. It put both front paws on her shoulders and looked solemnly into her face for several moments before his weight became too great and both girl and dog collapsed to the floor.

"Dos, you fatass, get off me," said Georgie, muffled, from beneath what looked remarkably like a black shag carpet. She conducted all the introductions like this, hidden from view. "Tash and Ocean, this is Dostoyevsky, and the useless one there is Pushkin. Dos is a Great Pyrenees and Pushkin is a toy spaniel. They are both ridiculous. Oh, and these are my dads, Harold Tanaka and Harold Szabo. Harolds, this is Ocean, my friend, and Tashya, my girlfriend."

Tashya went bright red but for the rest of the night couldn't stop beaming. I shook Harold Tanaka's hand, then Harold Szabo's, which involved some acrobatics in the tiny foyer whose square footage was primarily occupied by Georgie and Dostoyevsky. I petted Pushkin, then Dostoyevsky, who, after covering Georgie's face with his enormous tongue, obliged to rise. Georgie reappeared, gasping and wet.

"Don't just stand there," she said to us cheerfully. "Take off your shoes and come in."

The house was wider inside than it was outside; in fact it was two townhouses, the wall between them torn down. I hadn't known it was possible to own one property in the city, much less two. I marveled at the chandelier and brooded about my bank account while one of the Harolds showed us into the parlor for cocktails. He really said *parlor*. It was the first time I'd ever heard the word in real life.

The parlor was dark and formal, with a whole wall of books and forest-green armchairs. I seemed to be sinking deeper and deeper into mine, until my knees were at my chin. I couldn't stop looking around. We drank something complicated containing grapefruit juice, except for Harold Szabo, the lawyer, who was drinking a deep red wine from a dusty bottle. I sipped my drink slowly, dreary about the way that alcohol could ruin just about anything.

Harold Tanaka, the neurosurgeon, wanted to know all about Tashya and Georgie, and he seemed positively giddy. This left me free to squint at the gilded titles on the rows and rows of beautifully bound books and at the fine, dim light fixtures, the huge and heavy Persian rugs. I had always loved American homes, since real estate was so essentially American. I liked brokers' websites and home improvement shows, and the couches that stayed spotless though they weren't wrapped in squeaky plastic, and I was fascinated by the way everything from dinnerware to bath towels came in matched and monogrammed sets.

I couldn't believe people lived their whole lives in such houses, where the kitchen didn't stink of cooking oil. Nothing in my house matched; *everything* smelled like cooking oil. My life in my mother's house had been defined by a certain lack of control: loose papers and stacks of mail, old furnishings and an inadequate number of chairs. But Georgie's house was a different world entirely, though she too identified as middle-class. The chandelier light ricocheted and fractured off every surface until I was sure I was going blind.

"You don't like your drink," said Harold the lawyer. It took me several beats to realize he was talking to me. "Here," he said, before I could protest, or lie. Out of apparently nowhere, he produced another enormous wineglass and filled it half-way with his heavy red wine. Then he reached behind his armchair—into which he was sinking far less urgently than I seemed to be in mine—and came up with something that looked like a fire extinguisher, which he inserted directly into my wineglass. Something hissed and filled the glass to the brim, and when Harold handed it to me, I held it gingerly, like one might hold an angry, bristling cat.

"It's seltzer," he said, and then, "It's Hungarian." The whole interaction felt nonsensical. But I drank, and somehow it tasted like neither wine nor seltzer but both earthy and airy, almost pleasant.

Harold raised his glass to me, and we both drank deeply.

"By the way," said Georgie, "I've gone vegan again."

Georgie was forever trying to quit meat. She thought of all morality as a matter of willpower. Unfortunately, she was also the most carnivorous person I knew, and was always watching DiCaprio documentaries to convince herself otherwise. It was a delicate balance of opposing forces, like everything good in life, she explained to me one afternoon in our kitchen while gnawing on a chicken wing.

Both of the Harolds were deeply disappointed by Georgie's renewed veganism, as though she had told them she had recently been arrested, or decided to pierce her tongue. Harold the neurosurgeon looked genuinely pained as he turned back to his conversation with Tashya.

Tashya said, somewhat tiredly, that she was Slovenian, "like Donald Trump's wife." Harold the lawyer learned that his hometown was near Tashya's, and even knew that Tashya's town had quite a nice art festival. This perked Tashya up considerably, and they came to chat about this. Unfortunately, this meant the other Harold's attention fell to me. "So, Ocean, are you in school?

"She's on a gap year, Dad," said Georgie. "I told you."

"Ah, of course," said Harold, becoming animated, and for the next ten minutes he told us about how the other Harold had done his graduate degree at the same school I ought to have been attending. He got misty as he recounted the visits he would pay from California, where he was slogging through his own graduate degree, while Georgie rolled her eyes at me and picked at her cuticles. "But the campus will still be there in a year, of course. It's always good to take time to explore when you're young. The classrooms will keep."

He beamed at me. I tried to smile back. I couldn't think of a thing to say. Parents made me nervous.

"So why the gap year?" he asked. "An internship in the city?"

"Jesus, Dad," said Georgie. I was surprised by how angry she sounded, and how tense she got around her parents. "She's just taking a year off, okay? People are allowed to do that. There's no proper timeline for life, and not everyone has to go to school."

I felt a rush of affection for her and her anger. "I'm just taking some time," I ventured. What else could I say? That I had seen the undergrad suicide rates? That my neurology felt

THE CARTOGRAPHERS | 83

too fragile? "I'm looking for a job, though. Or an internship."

Georgie glanced at me, surprised. I hadn't told her yet about my humiliating résumé trek.

Harold the neurosurgeon frowned. "I hope Georgie hasn't been a bad influence on you. The college will still be there, of course, but it only matters if you *do* return to it."

For a second I was sure Georgie would snap. Instead she chugged her drink and went to make another. Harold looked like he was going to stop her, so I said quickly, "No, it's only a deferment. But in the meantime, I think it'd be good to get some real-world experience."

The real-world experience part seemed to please him. "What sort of work are you looking for?"

Georgie returned with a drink. She too looked at me expectantly.

"Well," I said, hesitant, "I used to work in a bookstore. But it seems like those are pretty in-demand jobs here. Everything is, really."

"You should tutor," said Georgie. "Everybody is always looking for a tutor. Dad, don't the Rothmans have a kid who's doing standardized testing soon? Did you know Ocean got perfect scores on all her tests?"

"That's very impressive, Ocean," said Harold approvingly. "I'll pass your number to the Rothmans, if that's something you're interested in. Georgie, I hope Ocean is a good influence on *you*."

"Of course," Georgie said sweetly.

While Harold was preoccupied taking down my contact information, she turned to me and stuck her middle finger up her nose.

At dinner we had clam pasta, which Georgie acquiesced to eat after a heated exchange with Harold the neurosurgeon that ended with Harold the lawyer slamming another bottle of dusty wine on the table and roaring, "Your father has been cooking all afternoon!"

Harold the neurosurgeon served the pasta with lemon that we had to juice with a ceramic knob Georgie had made in high school. It was hideous and extremely difficult to use, especially because as we passed it around the table Georgie kept trying to snatch it and throw it in the trash, which excited the dogs. I squirted lemon juice directly into my left eye. Both dogs seemed to think this was the funniest thing in the world. Harold the neurosurgeon scolded them while I stumbled, one-eyed, to the bathroom. Both dogs followed me and were difficult to discourage, especially Dostoyevsky.

After I'd cleaned my face as best I could with the fluffy bath towels, I checked the UNTITLED DOCUMENT. I had promised myself I wouldn't. I didn't want to seem rude in front of Georgie's parents.

I wasn't the only one in the document.

I stared in horror at the blinker, a different color than

mine, coming in and out of the document in sync with my heartbeat. I nearly threw my phone in the toilet. But before I could, the blinker began to move.

Ocean?

I didn't know what to do. I sat down on the closed toilet seat, stood up, sat again, stood again, and paced around the bathroom.

Constantine?

I sat down on the edge of the bathtub. He began typing back immediately.

Are you around?

Around where? In the amorphous cloud of the document? Here, still, on earth, or hell?

UWS, I wrote eventually.

Aha. Then there was a pause for such a long moment I thought the conversation was over. Finally he typed, Me too.

I worried for my heart, which seemed to be teetering on cardiac arrest. What did that mean? I wanted it to mean that *he* wanted to meet up somewhere; I wanted him to say that more than I'd ever wanted anything in my life. I felt this yearning for the document, like I had to physically lean into it. I felt foolish with hope, almost sick with it. The clam pasta was not sitting well.

There was a knock on the door that nearly startled me backward into the bathtub. "Ocean?" said Georgie. "Are you okay? I've been dispatched to offer you eye drops. Or antacids."

"I'm okay," I managed.

"Are you sure? You sound like you're being strangled."

That was exactly how I felt. "I'm not being strangled."

"If you say so."

She kept talking. I stopped listening. Constant was typing.

Will you meet me at the park?

Where? I wrote immediately. There was only one park he could mean, but how would I find him inside it, before the coyotes and rats found me?

72nd entrance. Can you be there in an hour?

I looked it up. I couldn't believe it was a real place, where I was going to meet him. My anxiety was jagged in my chest, but I didn't know why I should be so nervous, or why I could barely type because even my fingertips were clammy. Who was Constant, to make me so nervous? I looked at the document. *And so when you asked me if I was dead, you were really asking if we shared the same delusion, to which I say: yes.*

Be brave, I told myself, *like Constant.*

I think so.

I felt flimsy, like debris on a gale, at once curious and terrified as to where it would take me.

At the table, the dishes had been cleared and replaced with a tiramisu. The conversation had turned to consciousness. "But how do you *know* clams aren't conscious?" Georgie was saying. "Obviously a clam prefers to be left alone instead of harvested and poked at—you can tell when you prepare them, because you have to make sure they close up when you bother them. Doesn't that show, behaviorally, they *prefer* to be left alone?"

Tashya and I were both amazed. "When have you ever made clams?" Tashya asked.

Georgie ignored this. She waved her fork, splattering us in mascarpone. The dogs looked so hopeful.

"Indeed, what is it like to be a bat?" Harold the lawyer ruminated. "But, Georgie, we weren't really talking about consciousness. We were talking about your attention span, and how your dad and I need you to make some kind of commitment to your future."

"What future?" Georgie cried. "The Arctic is *gone*. The corporations own everything and you're protecting their rights! I don't want your dirty money, or Dad's. I don't want this ridiculous house, either. I want to live on a farm in Wyoming, and be a beekeeper, and make people laugh, and live with sixteen giant dogs."

Pushkin, improbably, whined at that very moment.

Georgie glanced at him. "Sorry, Push. But you'll probably be dead by then. Anyway, it's late, and the trains are stopping early tonight." This, for all I knew, might even be true. "We have to run, right now."

She glared at Tashya and me and grabbed the dish of tiramisu. We both jumped up.

"And who exactly is financing this Wyoming ranch?" Harold called after us.

"My world-renowned, highly in-demand, piano-soloist wife!" Georgie screamed, already heading for the door.

Tashya and I muttered our thanks to the Harolds and hurried after her. In the dim light, the two men looked exhausted, and very old. The dogs were fast on our heels, intent on keeping us from leaving. Georgie had to physically push Dostoyevsky out of the foyer. Somewhere along the way Tashya had become burdened with the tiramisu. Georgie, muttering expletives under her breath, ushered us into our coats and out the door.

Outside, it was chilly and silent. Georgie sat down hard on the top step of the stoop, took a deep breath, and screamed, "Fuck!" at the top of her lungs. Inside, the dogs started barking; and then all down the street, inside all the other townhouses, other dogs came to their windows until the whole block was agitated, and the barking reverberated off the buildings.

"Georgie," Tashya said faintly, clutching the tiramisu.

But Georgie was already back on her feet and tugging us along. "Come on, now we have to run. The Harolds will come out to yell at me."

She dragged us toward the train. My heart was in my throat. I had to go in the other direction, toward the park. I stopped. I didn't know what to say.

"Well?" Georgie said impatiently, looking back at me. "Come on."

"I—I actually . . . I actually have to go somewhere else."

"What?" cried Georgie. "Where are you going? Where do you have to go? Can we come? I've just been disowned, probably. Aren't we invited?"

Suddenly I felt helpless, and tired. My stomach was twisting tighter by the minute at the prospect of seeing Constant: I couldn't imagine it, and I couldn't imagine life after it. I felt like everything was about to change in some fundamental way. Georgie, who at first looked outraged, began to look concerned.

Tashya was considering my face so carefully I was sure she knew exactly what I was up to, and why. I thought she would try to stop me, but instead she tugged gently on Georgie's coat. "We have to get this tiramisu home," she said. "Stop bullying Ocean. She's put up with you enough for one night." Tashya leaned close and pecked me on the cheek. My chest suddenly contracted, and I felt close to crying. "Safe adventuring, Ocean. We'll see you in the morning," she said, like a blessing, and towed Georgie away.

I watched them until they turned the corner. Tashya directed Georgie along swiftly, but Georgie kept craning her neck back to stick out her tongue in my direction. At the intersection I heard them laughing; then they were gone.

HELL AND HIGH WATER

I found the park entrance with most of the hour to spare. It was getting dark, but the area was full of dogs and their walkers. I didn't know where to stand or what to do with my hands. I still had my copy of *The Little Prince*, but I didn't want Constant to find me reading a children's book. I didn't want to check my phone again, either. I was stressed about how often I checked the document, though of course this was the only reason we had collided earlier. I wanted him to write back more than I wanted to talk to any real person in my life, even Tashya and Georgie.

And then, there he was. I saw him while he was still several blocks away. He was taller than the piled-up trash, taller than anyone else on the sidewalk. I felt my cheeks go bright red. I knew I was an idiot. I was so happy to see him, and I was miserable. He got closer and closer. I forgot how to stand, where to look.

"Hi," he said when he reached me.

I wasn't sure he was real. His grin was so crooked. His jaw was stern and his cheekbones very high; his eyes were hooded and his eyebrows overly strong. Something about him was difficult and wonderful to look at, and the effect was illusory. I wanted to touch him, even just the corner of his jacket. I couldn't believe he was in front of me. I couldn't speak. I nodded at him.

Constant directed us deeper into the park. "I had an evening class," he said, with an air of explanation. "It was my seminar class, on determinism. Three hours in the basement every Thursday. The worst thing about philosophy is that every year you think the religious studies people have been weeded out, and every year there they are again. Why have a ration-based debate with someone having a religion-based debate? Why bother? I'd still recommend the class, though." He glanced at me. "You're a freshman, right? We're at the same school."

I tripped. My knees literally gave out; Constant had to catch my elbow to keep me from falling.

"I looked you up in the directory," he said, "just out of curiosity. I had a hunch that you were a student. You just looked so exhausted. I hope you don't mind."

I didn't know what to say. I didn't know I was in the directory. There must have been some mistake.

"But you live in Brooklyn . . . ," he mused.

I broke out in a sweat. I didn't know why I hadn't opened

my mouth to correct him yet, but what was I supposed to say? That I had taken a gap year on account of my suicidal tendencies, that I was afraid that if I went to school, I'd jump off the tallest building?

I said, "Well, the map isn't the territory."

Constant stopped walking. He looked down at me for so long I was sure I had said something really stupid. Then he nodded. "You're right," he said, and I felt both pleased and ashamed.

We started walking again. Constant was rummaging for something in his pockets, and I fully expected him to pull out spray paint. Instead he withdrew a wrinkled ziplock and a stack of rolling papers. He rolled a perfect joint as we walked into the dark. I couldn't stop staring at his fingers, which were longer and slimmer than mine, and so dexterous. I couldn't fathom how he rolled and walked at the same time. It didn't occur to me to panic until he handed me the joint by its perfect tapered end. Then he handed me a lighter.

The problem with language, and with being a person, was the set of rules and definitions you're already supposed to be familiar with. When Constant asked me to meet him at the park, he was really asking if I wanted to smoke, and by pure context I was supposed to have understood and consented to this. Now it was too late to turn back. We crossed into a meadow, and suddenly the city was as dark as I'd ever seen it. I felt like we had crossed into a slightly different reality. I felt Constant's attention on me, sharp; then it occurred to me that his attention was on the joint, which I was still holding in my damp fingers.

"I can't light it," I confessed.

I had only smoked once before, with Georgie, after she'd wheedled for a long time. It had felt different then, sitting on Georgie's bed in her cozy lighting as we mused about whether Tashya had feelings for her. I wasn't sure I'd gotten high, because I had only touched my lips to the joint long enough for her to stop badgering me. The circumstances now felt a thousand times more consequential. I couldn't stumble ten feet back to my own bed, for one thing, and I felt like I couldn't say no.

"That's okay," said Constant. "I can do it for you."

His hand was on my hand. It was just there, all of a sudden, enveloping mine. Because we were in such darkness, it felt intimate, as though I had done something vulnerable though I'd done nothing at all. I put the joint between my lips. He slipped the lighter from my hand and leaned over me. Then he was my entire world. He cupped his hands close to my face. His hands were really beautiful; it was difficult to breathe when he was so close to me, and he hadn't even lit the joint.

"Lean in," he said, and I did until there was no space between us. He flicked the lighter, and the flame stunned me though I knew to expect it. I breathed in, hard.

At once the smoke hit the back of my throat like I had swallowed flame. It was so painful it brought tears to my eyes, and I began coughing so violently I was worried I'd puke. He plucked the joint from my fingers and took a long, smooth inhale, and then another, and then another.

"Let's sit," he said.

I followed him, miserable, to a bench. I was coughing so hard I dropped *The Little Prince,* and Constant and I both tried to pick it up, fumbling around in the dark. The blood rushed to my head, so that when we were finally upright again I was dizzy, and fell almost sprawling onto the bench. Constant was looking at the book. I could see his frown. Wasn't it funny, I thought, that I had never really seen him in good lighting.

"This is *The Little Prince,*" he said, poking at the tattered wrapping. "But that's so strange. I was just trying to find my copy today, and then I remembered I sold it last year while I was moving out for the summer."

I stared at him.

"What?" he asked.

"I bought it today," I said, "from a used bookstore."

He sat down with the book in his lap. Then he looked at me, really looked into my face for the first time that night. There it was again—that cheerfulness that made him handsome. His hair was dark and longer than I remembered. I was aghast at how badly I wanted to touch it. He was so close; it would be so easy.

"Huh," he said. "Strange things seem to happen around you, Ocean."

He paged through the book. We found a note in the front, in elegant scrawl and fountain-pen ink: *To Adam and Alice. Grandma loves you.*

"Ah," said Constant. "I wonder who these people are."

The book looked really old. "They're probably dead," I said, glum. "Or they sold everything and moved to Florida."

Constant laughed. "Can I borrow it? I'll give it back the next time I see you."

The next time I see you. My rib cage squeezed tight around my lungs. I nodded.

Constant slipped the book into one of his pockets. He sprawled out on the bench, his head thrown back, and stared up at the six visible stars. I was starting to feel panicked in a way I'd never felt before. My whole body was heavy, like I'd been submerged in a slightly different version of things. I couldn't stop blinking.

Strange things seem to happen around you, Ocean. He had said it like a compliment. But then he handed the joint back to me, and then there was no more time to marvel at either improbability or determinism. I had to smoke again. Here was something no one had told me in those middle-school programs: no one offered you drugs for free unless they already cared about you. A joint was never just a joint. Everything meant something else, and refusing a joint was less about peer pressure and more about plain rudeness. I was happy and unhappy to be smoking with Constant, until I had to take another hit, and then I was only high, and couldn't stop thinking about how much my throat hurt.

I watched his chest move as he inhaled; I watched the glowing tip of the joint go closer and closer to his face, until he tossed it to the ground and crushed it under his heel. He threw back his head to billow out a long white stream of smoke. I wanted to reach out and touch him, his face, but I was afraid that my hand would close over nothing, over air.

"So," said Constant, "what other strange things have happened around you lately, Ocean?"

He always said my name on an exhale. When he said my name it sounded like breathing, and somehow this felt closer to the soul of my name than when anyone else said it, like he'd found some essential part of it often lost in English. And it *did* seem like many curious things had happened, all in a row: the enormous dog and the tiny one, the strange circumstances of *The Little Prince,* the concept of a cloud document, the fact of the internet, the way the earth fell through the universe at the same rate as my body from a great height.

"What if strange things happen around me because this is my dream?" I asked.

Constant grinned. I immediately worried that he, being a figment, would take this opportunity to disappear. Instead he took my hand. I was astonished, then subdued. His hand was rough and there was paint dried at his cuticles and at his wrist. His hand was so much larger than mine that he probably could have held my other hand too, like birds, in his long, tapered fingers. I felt a stab of despair. I adored his hands.

"So what?" he said. He said it kindly, but I flinched. "So what if it's a dream? There's no way to prove it's not. Ocean, Ocean, listen. If life and death are both so absurd that you can't tell the difference between them, then the difference doesn't matter. Only the absurdity matters. Don't you see? Eventually every reality is false. We might be simulated, or we might be dreaming, but you and I will probably never know. There's no leaving the matrix, so why waste time trying? The way I see it, we're in a lucid dream, you and I; we're waking dreamers. Maybe Sisyphus *liked* hiking. Let's have a hell of a time."

I didn't know what to say. I didn't feel understood, but I didn't want him to drop my hand.

"Come with me," he said, and I did.

Because I was high, it took me a long time to realize that we were going deeper into the park. I was horrified—*this* was consciousness? Being high made me feel more dead than ever. I could see rats dashing across our path, and distantly, other people like us, with complicated feelings. I looked up at Constant's wide back. I wanted to ask him about the document, about the things he said in it, and also why he had made it in the first place. Why didn't he ask for my phone number? I couldn't seem to open my mouth.

Suddenly it seemed like the document was the most fragile and precious thing that I had in my whole life. Talking about it out loud might corrupt it fundamentally. What if Constant wasn't real, and neither was the document? What if I mentioned it and all of it disappeared? Or what if I mentioned the document, and Constant stopped writing in it?

Constant was talking about Sisyphus again. "Most people live their lives as if death is an uncertainty. But death is the only certain thing—*life* is uncertain. Aren't we all like Sisyphus? At school on a bell schedule, like factory workers, Monday, Tuesday, Wednesday, Thursday, Friday, and then again after the weekend, not because we want to, but because we have to."

I plodded along after him, dead as a zombie, transfixed. He was right—everything felt like a nightmare.

"Meanwhile there are real things we have no intuition for," Constant said, "like the vacuum of infinite space or the order of time, and here we are still blundering along for this relentless economy, compelled to keep working. Nothing we do is meaningful; everything is headed toward oblivion. The world, if you look at it with reason, is an inhuman, foreign place. Then you realize—it's not *the world* that's essentially absurd, but this thing *reason*, this appetite we all have to understand something absolutely. But the world can't be reduced to rationality—that's why everything feels so absurd."

The trees parted. The sky was suddenly clear. The night was unduly beautiful—how could it be real? Constant looked at the sky and said, "Knowing all that, how can anyone keep going? Shouldn't we all just quit?"

Constant didn't understand. I was literally in hell. I hadn't arrived here by reflection, as he was suggesting. Though I agreed with him that the conditions of this life were brutally absurd, it seemed like we were in the minority. Most people were perfectly capable of being happy, making friends at school and work, living life, or getting out of bed in the morning.

I was in hell because I had almost certainly jumped off a water tower. It had happened after a fight with my mother. The problems I had with my mother were primarily ones of language, since we didn't speak a common one anymore. I was forgetting how to speak Chinese. Because my mother was the only one who spoke to me in Mandarin, I'd learned the language without context, in isolation. I heard the things she said to me differently than she might have meant them. Harsher. All hyperbole and sarcasm were lost on me. Forgetting a language was troubling—I became aware of holes in my consciousness. Words escaped me, one by one.

My whole relationship with my mother existed within this waning comprehension.

"I think I'm depressed," I told her the week after I graduated high school. She'd roused me to have breakfast with her before she went to work, then nagged me for sleeping so much.

"Why are you so tired?" she'd asked me. "You don't do anything all day, why are you so tired?"

When I said I was depressed, what she heard was "I'm lazy and ungrateful." Her face went white, then red, and then she launched into a barrage of questions that quickly turned scathing. Depressed? What did I have to be depressed about? Hadn't she worked hard every day of my life so that I had everything I needed, and a great many things I wanted, besides? How could I be depressed, when there were so many people who were less fortunate than me? The implication being that *she* was one of them—my mother, who had left behind her entire life and family and drudged away in variously undignified jobs so that I could live in the first world, with all the privileges it afforded.

Eventually she ran out of time and left for work. I got back into bed and hated myself for hating my mother. I hadn't asked to be brought into the world, or to be brought to America, but here I was anyway, miserable. Whose fault was that? I decided I might as well jump off the old water tower.

On the way, I had to get gas. I couldn't leave my mother with an empty tank, or anything else to worry about. I waited for the tank to fill, dazed and heavy. When I went to pay, a man tried to grope me.

I dodged him. "No, thank you," I said, for some reason.

"Fuck you," he said, unperturbed. "Go back to your own country."

The cashier didn't meet my eyes. I paid and left. No one even wanted me here, I thought. Why go through all this trouble? I drove to the tower.

I had been invited to climb the water tower once before, after junior prom, though none of us had made it to the top in our dresses and bare feet. The rest of my classmates haunted it often: it was the tallest spot in town, which made it thrilling, though there wasn't much of a view.

I was relieved to be done with high school and dreaded starting college in the fall. I hated school, even though I was a woman and an immigrant and ought to have only wonderful thoughts on education. As far as I could tell, I hadn't learned a single useful thing during my first thirteen years of school. I had only become accomplished at following directions and navigating bureaucracy. I could see that the school system was failing us essentially, since it connected almost no one to their proper passions, but I could do nothing to change this, or any other fundamental problem I had identified in the world.

At the water tower, I parked on the street. The way up was wonderful, as I imagined the Tower of Babel or the Penrose stairs to be thrilling, just to climb and climb. I rose higher and higher. The water tower was a good place to trespass because you could see all the way to the police station and all of the approaching roads. I was crying as I climbed, but my hands weren't sweating at all. Soon my head would stop spinning; this was thrilling too.

At the top I stood at the railing and time fell away like shedding skin. I could understand why people, for most of human history, had thought the earth was flat. Before me was everything I knew. My whole town, the neighborhood I'd just left, though I couldn't pick out our individual house, and there, indeed, easy to keep an eye on, was the police station. The whole known world, flat as a map before me. I could jump right into it. I could dive headfirst and hit the ground so fast I would go straight to hell. It seemed so simple.

It was cloudy, and the sun was moving to a different part of the planet. I couldn't feel the tips of my fingers or toes, even though it was summer. In hindsight I couldn't say why I was so distraught, but I would remember the feeling forever: cleaved at the chest, full of salt water.

It was useless to dwell on the fact that the material conditions of my life were good—great, even. For the first time my mother had made us lower middle-class: we owned the house we lived in, we could buy things at eye level in the grocery store instead of searching the top or bottom shelves for cheaper brands, we paid off all our credit cards. I had gotten into a good school, and I didn't even have to bury myself in debt to attend. Despite all this I felt an absence where there ought to have been some will to live. I couldn't explain this to my mother. I couldn't explain it to anyone. Every day was such a dead end, and I was exhausted from banging my head against it. And then every morning I had to wake up and do it all over again. I didn't care anymore about what came after this life, any more than I cared about what had come before it. I felt so undone it seemed only sensible to finish the job off.

I sat at the top of the tower all afternoon. Time passed quickly, then slowly, as I sat there. I hadn't eaten that morning, or much the day before. I sat there for so long I fainted, my legs still hanging over the edge.

I had only fainted once before, at a tennis practice during a heat wave, on a day I'd forgotten my water bottle and we were running suicides. But I often felt light-headed and once in a while, when this coincided with heat or panic, I became aware of my consciousness as it ebbed away. But on the tower, my legs dangling over a hundred feet of open air, there were none of these warnings. Maybe I'd cried too much; maybe I'd climbed too fast. But all of a sudden, I was waking up with my cheek pressed against damp metal, in complete darkness.

I was on my back, my neck at a funny angle on the narrow walkway. Above, the sky was clear and rounded, cluttered with starlight. Directly above me was the constellation Boötes, who turned the sky. When I sat up, my legs were still hanging over the edge.

I didn't remember climbing down at all. Maybe I had been in shock, or maybe it was just dark, and I was shaken. But now, whenever I thought about it, this seemed an aspect of the afterlife: my descent into hell, a blank space in my memory, the way that in a dream you could move from one moment to the next as easily as scenery changed on a stage, and everything could disappear without explanation.

Because I didn't know what else to do, I went home. The house was dark; my mother had gone out. In my room I found a plate of sliced fruit she'd left for me, browning in their own juices.

Constant led me to the river. "I thought we could take the ferry," he said.

I stared at him, dismayed. Didn't he know that my problems were real ones—problems I cared about literally, and not metaphorically? What if I had jumped off the water tower, and the fainting was a false memory? What happened to the park? How had the rest of it passed in such a blur? Now we were here, on the water. Why was he trying to put me on a ferry, while talking about hell? We arrived at a dock.

A boat appeared, as if out of nowhere, followed by a transportation employee. "Tickets," he demanded.

At the same time, Constant said to me, "My girlfriend—my once and future girlfriend—she hates the ferry, because she is deathly afraid of water."

The MTA employee turned to me, waiting for the tickets. I had lost all language. Had he just said *girlfriend*? I was mortified and didn't know what to do with my face. Constant pulled out his phone and showed it to the transportation employee, proffering two tickets. *So he does have a phone,* I thought dully. Then I had a terrible thought: was that the reason we only communicated through the UNTITLED DOCUMENT—because he had a girlfriend?

My once and future girlfriend. For a brief, elated moment I'd thought he meant *me*. But I was not deathly afraid of water. Was the emphasis on *once*, or on *future*, or on *girlfriend*? It seemed like an important distinction. I realized that we were just friends. It was a plummeting, seasick feeling. Why wouldn't Constant have a girlfriend? I felt so dumb. Of course we were just friends.

So, we were in hell. Only in hell would Constant already have a girlfriend. On the deck, there was a wonderful, clean breeze. I began to shiver. Now the beautiful night was ominous—like Constant was ferrying me through an illusion. I was so sure that when the boat crossed the water, the astonishing city would dissolve. I was dejected and humiliated as he ushered me to the top deck, then the bow. And there was the whole city, rising on either side of the river, the glittering towers as far as I could see. Nothing was real. Constant was talking about the Styx. I felt tears pricking my eyes. So this was it, I thought, the point of no return—he would take me across limbo, and from here on out things could only grow worse.

"Sisyphus had the right idea," Constant continued, "because he realized that there could be no ethics if the gods were just as silly as the rest of us. They punished him, for proving it, but he was right in the end. The afterlife is full of the same bullshit as earth."

"Everything you say makes sense to me," I said, "but you always come to a different conclusion than I do. Like that first email you sent me, about the train. I thought that was about losing yourself, about how over a lifetime you shed habits and replace them with new ones, you make friends and you lose them. And through it all the only thing that stays the same is the name of the thing, the particular train, though everything else has changed. I thought you were say-ing something about this . . . self." I didn't know where I was going or why I was still talking. I was miserable, and I couldn't look Constant in the face. "About how we think of ourselves as consistent people, even though it's not *reasonable* to think so. Though the only thing that stays constant is memory, and experience—the feeling of being in your own body. But that's not what you were talking about, was it? You were talking about the MTA."

I had more to say, about Sisyphus, but couldn't say it. My throat had closed. *Why are you telling me this?* I wanted to ask. I already knew it was better to be content with this life than to be despairing, but how could I help it? How could he sit there and tell me to be happy because *nothing* had meaning?

Beneath us, the motor came on, and the boat began pulling away from the dock. He handed me his windbreaker. All my joints went soft. Constantine, who could talk for hours and write on and on without really listening. All it took for me to forgive him was the jacket off his shoulders, still warm from his chest.

Look at him. Of course he had a girlfriend—once, or in the future.

"Well," he said. He folded his hands across his knee, in a way that communicated thoughtfulness. "The thing about a train that makes it a particular train—what makes the C train the C train, I guess, isn't the train itself. It's the route it runs, or the stops it makes. The C train running on the F line is an F train, but an R32 and an R188 can both be C trains."

I didn't know how to respond. Once again he had sidestepped what I was really trying to ask him.

"Sisyphus was the same in life and in hell," he said, "and his consciousness was the same too, just as hideous. He was still on the same route, stuck in the same vicious cycle. So maybe . . ." He turned to me and gripped my shoulders. His palms were hot, and a rush went through my whole body. "Maybe *it's not important*. Of course life is absurd, but we have to imagine that Sisyphus was having a good time. Maybe he *likes* hiking. Maybe the view is great."

I heard this with a sinking feeling. But *I* was having a hideous time. That was what I was trying to tell him.

The ferry bounced between Queens and Manhattan. At each stop I held my breath and waited for the illusion to dissolve. The city remained, but I wasn't convinced. Constant went on about Sisyphus's rock and how our burdens always found us. He kept talking, though I had nothing to say in response. "The struggle itself toward the heights is enough to fill a man's heart," he quoted. Maybe for Constant, I thought, or Camus. What about my heart?

"Is it my turn to write to you?" Constant asked. "Or yours to write to me?"

"Mine," I said.

"Okay," said Constant. "In that case, I hope many improbable things happen to you before we meet again."

"You too," was all I could think of to say.

He smiled at me. "Nothing strange happens to me, except around you."

"Funny," I said. "I was thinking the same thing about you."

"Ah," he said. The grin. "Then we must see each other again."

In no time at all the ferry found its way to Midtown, then Brooklyn. Constant stuck his hands in his pockets. He smiled at me. I couldn't believe I was still high; I wanted to shake it off, like water from my ears. There was still so much I wanted to say to him. I was touched that he had seen me back to Brooklyn, and devastated that he was leaving me here.

"I'll just take this back up," he said, of the ferry. I thought about how Charon too, dropped the dead on the shores of the Styx without ever stepping foot off the boat.

"Write me fast," he said, "and see you soon."

I got to my feet. He waved his whole arm, until I had to turn my back on him and walk off the top deck of the ferry. Loneliness doused me. I felt my knees giving out. The whole way home I could think of nothing but that Rilke quote, about how love consisted of two solitudes bordering and saluting each other, and how beautiful this sounded, and how miserable I felt.

WORD GAMES

Overnight it was fall. Some of the trees managed to turn yellow before an ice storm came and in one weekend tossed all their leaves to the ground in sodden, dirty piles. It started raining almost every day, and the meager light that used to seep down to my alley-facing window vanished. I started sleeping for nine or ten, then twelve or thirteen hours a day. Even inside I could sense my part of the world growing colder and moving out of the sun.

My mother called me about Thanksgiving. Georgie had invited both me and Tashya to the Harolds' for Thanksgiving dinner, and we had all decided to stay in the city for the break. Tashya didn't go home to Slovenia except for a month of winter. I, of course, couldn't go home. It was one thing to lie to my mother on the phone once a week, to say that my classes were going well, but I couldn't do it to her face. I couldn't make up professors' names or friends. The idea of going back to my town seemed like inviting bad luck; I couldn't do it. I really tried to imagine how I could make it work, though, because the thought of my mother spending Thanksgiving alone made my heart feel like it was turning inside out. I'd hated holidays growing up because it was almost always just the two of us, and I couldn't shake the image of my mother eating in our kitchen alone.

But she took the news much better than anticipated. It turned out that she'd turned down a trip to California with some friends so that I could come home and eat turkey, though neither of us liked turkey. Now that she could go to California, she planned to have duck instead, with better sides. I hung up feeling oddly miffed. I was relieved my mother's life without me was not as bleak as I'd imagined it, but nonetheless I felt abandoned.

Days passed, one after the other. I couldn't think of a single thing to write. I thought if I waited long enough, Constant might explain either the girlfriend or his thoughts on existentialism. Again and again I read his last paragraph, which seemed to have soured as it aged. *The same delusion,* I read, then thought, *once and future girlfriend.* For hours on end I sat in my bed and thought about the time we'd spent together, my memory of which felt strange and uncertain, like trying to recall a dream you were already forgetting. Was that quality a thing that belonged to me, or Constant, or the weed? There was no way to know. I thought about his girlfriend so much that she began to appear in my dreams.

For some reason, she looked just like Tashya but blond. In the dream I was paralyzed on a subway bench, watching as she and Constant boarded the train hand in hand, while she tossed her hair and laughed and never looked at me directly.

I had my first job as a tutor. I was really nervous, and exhausted from staying up all night scouring the internet for tips on tutoring for different standardized tests. I was so worried about falling asleep during the session I caved and spent seven dollars on a coffee that was mostly milk foam.

On the train everything reminded me of Constant. Every tall person in a long coat looked like him. I wondered what would happen if I never wrote to him again. How long would I have to wait before he reached out? Or would we just forget each other, each of us swallowed by the city, until even the subway tunnels stopped reminding me of him? I couldn't imagine forgetting him, or moving on. The subway had become hopelessly entangled with Constantine Brave from the moment he waved at me across the platform.

The Rothmans' apartment building had two doormen: one who stood outside and waved me in, and another who sat by the elevators in the largest and most ornate lobby I'd ever seen in real life. The ceiling was painted like the Sistine Chapel, and all the picture frames were gilded. I almost walked into a mirror because my neck was craned back. The mirrors were gilded too.

When I got upstairs, the nanny let me in. She was a little older than me and only spoke French. Behind her was a six- or seven-year-old, who I hoped was not my pupil, working on a puzzle. By pointing at various doors, the nanny communicated to me that the mother was on a conference call in the home office. Then she led me to a fourteen-year-old, Benny, whose bedroom had a view of Central Park.

"Benny is," said the nanny, and flapped her hands while she searched for the word, "very timid, yes?"

Timid was a generous word for Benny. Despite being fourteen, he was no taller than Georgie and thin as tissue paper. His hair was bright orange, and I saw a lot of it because he never once looked up at me. Instead he sat at his desk and I sat at a chair next to his desk, and for an hour and a half I ran vocabulary flash cards with him while he answered in a reedy mumble.

"Abstruse," I read.

"Difficult to understand," said Benny, in such a low register it was, indeed, difficult to understand.

"Circumlocution."

"To talk about something indirectly."

"Duplicity," I said.

"Deceiving, or acting in bad faith."

I shuffled the flash cards so they would stop describing my life. My days were filled with abstruse conversation consisting entirely of circumlocution. All of it occurred under the duplicitous umbrella of my circumstances in the city. The next card I drew was *epistolary*.

"Written in the form of letters, or correspondence," said Benny. I felt unreasonably annoyed at him. To put an end to the flash cards, I had Benny practice reading comprehension questions. The first passage we turned to was from Borges's "On Exactitude in Science," which was about a country that drew a map so detailed it became as large as the country itself.

At precisely the ninety-minute mark, there was a knock on the door. Benny's mother entered wearing yoga clothes. She had that youthful glow of wealth. Her name was Olivia, she said, shaking my hand vigorously, and she was sorry she hadn't been there to greet me. There had been some kind of disaster in her buyers' department involving a misplaced decimal.

"We're so glad Harold recommended you," she kept saying. "We've been in such dire need."

"That's not what dire means," said Benny, speaking up for the first time.

Olivia thought this was hilarious. She handed me an envelope full of money and made Benny tell me he couldn't wait to see me again the following week. Somehow I was rushed, very politely, out of the apartment and deposited on the doormat.

On the elevator I counted the cash. I'd made two hundred and fifty dollars. I wondered if Olivia knew about all the different flash-card apps online, most of which were free.

• • •

On the ride back to Brooklyn, I wrote to Constant. I couldn't help myself. I was thinking about things I didn't know how to express to anyone in the world, except him.

In Borges's version of "On Exactitude of Science," the country eventually abandons their enormous map, but in Baudrillard's version the country crumbles and the people move *into* the map, so that the map indeed becomes the territory. Living in the twenty-first century feels like living in this map that corresponds to nothing: our lives are so removed from reality. Urbanization has moved us out of nature, and the US dollar hasn't been backed by gold since 1933. Even our conversations happen in a cloud, which is really a computer farm in some desert out west. When I tell you I think I'm in hell, I mean it literally. I think I really did jump off that water tower. Sometimes it's even easier for me to think I'm dead than to believe that everyone else is also enduring such absurd and awful things. If I'm not dead, then why isn't life improving? Do you mean these things that you write to me? How can anyone *mean* anything at all?

It seems to me that the way we talk to each other is like Sisyphus's boulder—the thing he can't escape. Every day I feel less able to be objective, or to be sure what's real. I don't feel in control of what I do or what I write. What if language is holding us back, us especially—what if by talking to each other, we're actually dooming ourselves? How can Sisyphus be happy, just because hell is also absurd? Are we doing ourselves a disservice to imagine him happy, just because Camus told us so? Are we even writing to each other, or just shouting into the void? Do you really have a girlfriend?

To my great surprise, our fake IDs arrived. They came in the false bottom of a jewelry box containing a tangle of cheap bangles. They were made of too-thick plastic and didn't look real at all, though Georgie assured me that they would scan and most bouncers didn't care anyway. In my photo I looked at least twenty-five, with dark circles under my eyes and a really dead look. I wondered if the photograph revealed something true about me.

"Wow," Georgie said. "You look ancient. This is the best ID I've ever seen." I liked the bangles a lot more than the ID. Georgie said I could keep them.

That same weekend Georgie gave up on her dreams of being a touring comedian and decided to pursue her true passion of selling small-batch clay earrings online. "Of course, it kind of directly opposes my views of this late-capitalist market," she mused, "but since I'm not contributing to global deforestation by way of factory farming right now, I can afford to be a little immoral in other ways." She'd said this at dinner; Tashya and I were eating frozen beef tamales. For weeks our kitchen was full of fumes from the polymer clay baking in the air fryer, but we couldn't open any of the windows because of the rain.

MIND THE GAP

I started seeing a lot of signs I was in hell. All the news was disastrous. At Benny's the next week, we had the lesson in the living room, with the ambient noise of the TV in the background. For ninety minutes, different anchors reported on awful things from all over the world. In Tibet, several sherpas died in an avalanche. South Africa was running out of water—the anchor held up a calendar that read DAY ZERO, then the camera panned over several parched-looking communities. It seemed to be a really bad week for bees. Several parts of the world were even literally on fire: there were scenes of black clouds and flames from correspondents in California, Australia, Brazil.

While Benny did practice questions, I couldn't tear my eyes away from the screen, until the news itself seemed really strange. Like why did all anchors have perfectly symmetrical faces? Why was there a banner scrolling across the bottom of the screen with even more news that was not *as* bad as the news that got airtime, but appalling nonetheless? Why did all channels use the same serious font? It was as though everything was designed to convey that this was the unfiltered truth. I started to feel seriously suspicious.

Then I was walking home on the first critically cold day. A bent old lady leaned out from her ninety-nine-cent store to wave a blue glass charm at me. I wanted to stop and ask her what she saw in me: was I dead? Had I jumped? Could she tell me? But as soon as I slowed down, she waved the evil eye harder and started yelling at me in a language I couldn't identify.

When I made it back to the apartment, Georgie gasped when she saw me. "Oh my god," she said. "Did you get mugged?" She dragged me in front of a mirror. At some point, my nose had started bleeding; it did this sometimes when the temperature fell. The blood had soaked all down the front of my coat.

There were devils everywhere. I ordered a coffee that came in a plastic cup emblazoned with a ghost holding a red pitchfork. Right after that, I noticed that all of the pedestrian walk signs had sprouted horns. I couldn't believe my eyes. I looked at it for so long the light changed again. It turned out to be some kind of prank that really panicked the city, because it was an impressive feat of hacking.

It was Halloween. At home, Georgie was wearing a headband with flimsy, sequined red horns. She had on a very short skirt and a pair of painful-looking go-go boots.

"They're Prada," she said. "Get it?"

"Groundbreaking," I told her.

Georgie treated Halloween very seriously. We were going to christen our new IDs. She frog-marched me to her room and made me look through several of her past ensembles. I was sure none of them would fit me, but Georgie wouldn't be discouraged. I ended up as Dorothy, from *The Wizard of Oz*, in a tight plaid dress. I had to hold my breath to pull it over my rib cage.

In the bathroom, Georgie caked a dozen products on my face and hair. "This is how much concealer I had to use to cover your under-eye circles," said Georgie, showing me the bottle and measuring with her fingernail. "You've *got* to start hydrating, Ocean." Then she towed me out the door, determined to pour alcohol, a dehydrator, down my throat.

We went to a lesbian bar where the ceiling was completely covered in fire hazards: hanging baubles and string lights, puppets and paper lanterns. No one looked at our IDs. Tashya was already there, waiting for us, dressed head to toe in black.

"You're not wearing a costume!" Georgie said, indignant.

Tashya looked down. "I'm a pianist."

She had already gotten drinks, which appeased Georgie. I hadn't eaten much that day, so the tequila went straight to my head. I checked my phone under the table. It had been nearly a week since I'd written Constant, and he still hadn't responded. Nothing had been deleted, either.

Georgie leaned over my shoulder. "Who are you texting?"

I shut my phone off. "No one," I said.

She asked again after a third round of drinks. The alcohol had made Georgie wheedling and doe-eyed, but it only made me tired and sad, and certain I'd crossed some line with Constant. I shouldn't have asked him about his girlfriend, and then I thought, of course I should have. What else was language for? Nonetheless I didn't feel ready to tell Georgie and Tashya about Constant. I didn't want to say his name out loud; it felt unlucky, like I might accidentally summon him. There was something tender and amorphous between Constant and me, something likely to evanesce as easily as it had appeared. It felt like a disservice to put anything that had happened into words, to say them to anyone but Constant. Besides, there were all sorts of details about our correspondence that would raise eyebrows: the graffiti, the way I only seemed to see him at night and in strange circumstances, the fact that we had never texted or talked on the phone but communicated through a cloud document without a name. But Georgie wouldn't let up.

"Has anyone ever . . . ," I tried, and then felt such pressure at the center of my chest I had to stop talking. The feelings I felt were too big for words, or for me. I wanted to know what to do, and why Constant always deleted the things we wrote, and what it meant to fall in love with someone who loved someone else. Instead I said, "Do you know anything about metaphysics?"

"Metaphysics?" Georgie looked at me like I was crazy. I rubbed my nose, to make sure it wasn't bleeding.

"Like, existentialism," I said. The expression on Georgie's face suggested I had said something absurd, like "non-fungible token" or "decaf coffee." She and Tashya exchanged a look, and I wondered if I'd lost my mind. "I mean," I continued, "you hear about things like general relativity, or even that the earth is round, and you think, all the rest of this is bullshit. Language and money and politics, like all of it is just there to make it easier for us to live in giant, overpopulated communities. But none of it really means anything. Everything is just a symbol for something else. The word isn't the thing, and a map isn't the territory. What if they're doing more harm than good? What if the gap between the real thing and the representation of the thing is farther apart than we think?"

Georgie took my drink and peered into it. "You got us all the same thing, right?" she asked Tashya. She patted my face. "Are you feverish?"

"I'm serious," I said. The tequila was making my tongue all the wrong kinds of loose. "How do you know what's real?"

Georgie gave me my drink back. "Drink up. Then you won't care about . . . metaphysics."

But that was the problem, I wanted to tell her. The alcohol made everything waver more, and in the morning all the problems were back, and I felt even more troubled by how it *could* make me care less, like even the most essential parts of me were inconsistent. It felt hard to breathe in the din of the bar, which made me feel overwhelmed and distant from myself at the same time. I said, "Isn't it just crazy that at any moment, someone somewhere is liable to make some discovery that changes the meaning of everything? Every single thing about our lives? Einstein found out that space isn't empty; that changes *everything*. And yet life goes on. It takes us decades or centuries to even comprehend what he did. At any moment, the news could break—someone will come up with something that makes everything we believed before fundamentally wrong. That makes it feel like reality isn't fixed. But it is. We're the ones who aren't fixed."

Georgie was bewildered. "Is this because I dressed you up as Dorothy?" she demanded. She flicked me on the forehead.

"*Ow*," I said.

"See? It's not a dream."

I wasn't sure what she was trying to prove. I'd had plenty of painful dreams.

But Tashya was looking at me like she understood. In fact she looked so sad and knowing I felt sure she had deduced something I was trying to hide, and I couldn't bear to meet her eyes.

"Why do we drink?" I asked Georgie instead.

"Because life is unbearable," she said, but she said it languorously, stretching her feet onto Tashya's lap. Tashya put her hand on Georgie's ankle, so easily it made my chest do a funny little spasm, and I had to look away. "Oh, Ocean, because it's *fun*. Because it makes it easier to talk, and dance, because it makes you forget about the parts of yourself you don't like."

I still remembered all the parts of myself I didn't like. Now that we were on the subject, I couldn't stop thinking about the way I struggled to talk when I felt even the least bit panicked, the way I seemed to be capable of nothing but sleep, my lack of an opinion about anything at all.

Miserable, I said, "But why is life unbearable?"

Georgie laughed so hard that her margarita came out of her nose. She leapt upright and threw an arm around my neck, nearly sending us both toppling out of the booth. "Oh, Ocean, dear nihilist," she said. She smacked a kiss on my cheek. She too was drunk; but it felt so good to be held by someone I sank into her. "Who cares if life is unbearable, if we can bear it?"

It was roundabout logic, but she did have a point. Constant had said the same thing.

In the morning I was so hungover I could only see out of one eye for several minutes after I woke up. I felt bodily delicate, like one wrong lurch would send me vomiting, and I was so dehydrated I could feel my fingerprints. I got into the shower and dry-heaved for several minutes straight, until it felt like my lungs were trying to climb out of my body, unable to stand being trapped inside. Every rib hurt. I stood there until the water ran cold, and even then it was a serious effort to coordinate my limbs so that I could climb out and dry off, and collapse back in my bed.

I checked the untitled document. My paragraph was there, which I couldn't bear to read; I wanted to delete the whole thing. I would have, if I could be sure Constant had seen it already. Then I remembered I could check.

I went into the document's history before I could change my mind. I was already ashamed to be doing what I was doing, but it was too late: there it was. He had been in the document just last night, when I was sitting in a lesbian bar thinking about him. Before that he'd logged into the document twice: once at 2:07 on Thursday morning and once the evening I'd written, just moments after I'd finished.

He was never going to write back. He was going to disappear on me.

I felt panicked again, for wanting something I couldn't have. It felt awful to be so desperate. I would take ten or twenty more hangovers for him to appear in the document right now. Then I was ashamed, and tried to tell myself I didn't mean it. He could still write back. I hated myself for thinking it, but I couldn't shake the tiny hope, like a splinter that had grown into my skin.

Before I could change my mind, I deleted the paragraph I'd written. *Do you really have a girlfriend?* was the first sentence to disappear, letter by letter, but the rest quickly followed. There was a lump in my throat that made it hard to swallow. I felt like *I* was being swallowed.

The temperature plummeted. All the rats disappeared. The subways seemed more crowded than ever as everyone donned layer after layer. I had to get a new coat since my old one was splotched brown with nosebleed. When the cold became unbearable, Tashya and I shivered our way to the nearest thrift store and pawed through racks of questionable clothing, wrapping paisley scarves around our necks until we itched. In the coat section, everything was either extra small or extra large.

I had lost all hope. The untitled document was now blank except for Constant's map, taking up the whole first page. I'd looked at it so often that I almost never had to use my GPS to get around anymore. Constant's design was so easy to read that I had memorized almost all the places where different lines intersected or swerved close enough to walk between. On nights when I couldn't sleep, which was all of them, I ran all the stations of a line through my head, uptown to downtown, then back again: Eastchester-Dyre, Baychester, Gun

Hill Road, Pelham Parkway, Morris Park. Flatbush Avenue, Newkirk Avenue, Beverly Road.

It was no cure for insomnia. I couldn't stop thinking about Constant, what he was doing at that very moment. Could he really disappear on me? *Write me fast,* he'd said, *and see you soon.* Hadn't he meant it? Had he meant it until I'd asked about the sometimes girlfriend? Or had he been saying things he didn't mean this whole time?

"Tash," I said, then hesitated. I was about to ask, "How do you know if someone likes you?" But what I really wanted to know was: how do you know what is true?

I was silent for so long Tash came around from her side of the coat rack and squinted at me. "Ocean, are you all right?" she asked.

I was fine, I wanted to say to her. But I couldn't. Everything I said lately seemed either false or incomplete or inadequate. I didn't have enough vocabulary; Benny's vocabulary flash cards had only exacerbated the issue. In the end I just shrugged.

Tashya pressed her lips together. "Well," she said slowly, "the thing is, lately, it seems like you can't carry a conversation. And it looks like you're not sleeping at all, though you are sleeping all day."

I flipped miserably past a dark gray peacoat, which reminded me of Constant, and then a windbreaker, which also reminded me of Constant.

"You don't seem well," said Tashya gently. She held up a black parka for me to inspect, though the arms would have been short even on Georgie. Tashya was good at things like this—mildly interspersing criticism with something like coat buying, so I could occupy my hands while the blows fell. At any rate, she was doing a much better job than my mother, who had given me a similar speech before I climbed the water tower—about how I was not well and not grounded in reality.

"I think," I said. It was hard to get the words out. I leaned into the coats and closed my eyes. Everything smelled like mothballs. "I think it's possible that this is just an aspect of my being."

"Ocean, what does that even mean?"

It meant that it was in my stars to be miserable, prone to panicking, tired, and sickly because of it. It meant that all my life I had been a little lonely and a little glum, and it seemed I would be so for the rest of it; it meant that the problem was not with language but with me. This was the life I was stuck with, in a body I could not leave.

I thought if I moved to New York City, if I deferred college for a year and kept away from these larger anxieties, I would stop being such a miserable person. It was terrible to be suicidal. It was dull and repetitive, and it made you and your life the opposite of interesting. But here I was, and nothing was better; everything was worse.

Tashya sighed. She gathered me out of the coats and hugged me, briefly, with her whole body. She took me by the shoulders and shook me once, looking at me hard. "Is this about the philosopher?"

"What?" I was sure I had never mentioned Constant.

"The other night, when you asked if we knew anything about metaphysics," she said. "Well, you're talking to someone who *does*, right? Someone is filling your head with these grand theories, like general relativity, and meaninglessness."

I felt backed into a corner. I felt trapped by all the coats.

"You don't have to say who," said Tashya. "I just mean— look, Georgie and I have both been on dating apps too, okay? It's just awful, isn't it, how high the highs are, and how low the lows? It really makes you feel like you're losing your head, like someone's stuffed you in a dryer. Look, the thing is, when you're meeting someone online, there are . . . just too many gaps."

She thought I was on a dating app. I felt my cheeks burning. But what were Constant and I doing that was so different? *Too many gaps.* Too many days waiting for Constant to respond, reading the document's edit history like it could tell me something meaningful. Too many gaps in me too, like all the waiting and anxiety had worn me thin, full of holes in my memory and my sense of self.

"There's all this information missing, when you're meeting someone on a screen," she continued. "Things that feel

too nosy or desperate to ask. So you make do with not knowing for now, but there's so much information missing that
you end up putting too much importance on the things you
do know. You end up giving too much meaning to these little
signs that they like you, or don't like you. Like, what does it
mean if they take too long to text you back? The truth is, it
could mean anything, since you don't actually *know* anything
about their everyday lives. All you can do is deduce subtext.
But in real life, subtext is bullshit. It shouldn't be this convoluted game to figure out what feelings are real."

My head spun. But Constant and I hadn't met on a screen,
I wanted to insist. We had met in real life, on a night that
felt like a dream; in that sense, the document felt more real
than the time we had spent together, because I could refer
back in the document's edit history. I could look at our letters for proof.

But then what Tashya was saying hit me. What *did* I
know about Constant? I knew that he painted maps where
he shouldn't. I knew he was from Jersey, and I knew his dad
was a nuclear engineer, and his grandfather was a hoarder. I
knew what school he attended and what he studied, and I
knew he had a class on determinism every Thursday evening
in a basement. What else? That couldn't be it; that couldn't
be all the things I knew. But then I could only think about
the things I *didn't* know: how old he was, what he did when
he wasn't writing to me, who his friends were, what books he

read, if he had any pets. I didn't even know if he actually had a girlfriend; it was really unclear.

But . . . wasn't that what I liked about him? The way we had the same doubts about reality? The suspicion with which he regarded the world? It wasn't something you noticed right away in him—the suspicion. It hid under his cheerfulness. But it was there, and he seemed to understand me in a way that no one else did. Maybe I *liked* this convoluted game, because the rest of my life was so convoluted that it was the only language I could understand. Maybe that was exactly why I had such a propensity toward misery; maybe that was the greatest sign of all that I was in hell, and deserved to be.

"Look." Tashya sighed. "I just worry that you'd fall for someone like Thomas Sato."

I was stung. "What's that supposed to mean?"

"Well," said Tashya, "you know, like, the theory bros." She said "theory bros" in the same tone people said "spilled sewage" or "vomit in the rideshare." "You know what I'm talking about? Boys with all these grand ideas from books they've skimmed just to have something clever to say, who make you feel smart while reminding you they're smarter."

My stomach twisted. I could feel my nausea on my face.

"How about this one?" Tashya held a coat out to me when my silence had stretched for too long. The coat was enormous and a striking yellow; had I been a foot taller and in possession of a more vogue nose, it might have been sort of chic.

Instead, when I zipped it up and put on the hood, I looked like a bottle of mustard.

"I think it's the best I'm going to do," I said.

Tashya sighed. "See, Ocean," she said, "that attitude is most of your problem."

To cheer me up, Georgie gave me a pair of horseshoe-shaped earrings made of what looked like Play-Doh. They were hideous: badly marbled, rough at the edges, covered all over with Georgie's fingerprints. I adored them. I wore them every day for a week, though they clashed terribly with my new coat, until even Georgie begged me to wear something else.

ANIMALS

The world, Constant wrote, does not speak. Only we speak. It was the thirteenth day. Outside, the rain had turned to snow. In the space I had cleared for him, he had typed a dense, complicated paragraph I couldn't make sense of, even after I'd read it three or four times.

He wrote mostly about insects, or maybe free will. A wasp, he wrote, kills a cricket and carries it back to her nest. She'll lay her eggs next to the carcass so the baby wasps will hatch beside a full meal. But before she drags it home, she has to check that the nest is safe. In she goes to look it over. Outside, a scientist moves the cricket a few inches away. The wasp comes back to see that something has meddled with the cricket, so she checks the cricket to make sure no one has taken a bite of her food. Then she has to go inside and check the nest again, to make sure no wily predator has snuck in while she was distracted. In she goes again. The scientist moves the cricket again. The wasp comes back out, and the whole thing starts over.

It turned out the wasp would repeat this cycle forever, even if the scientist moved the cricket a hundred times. Constant didn't like what this said about free will, since it was clear the wasp had some sort of compulsion that would trap it in this loop for as long as the scientist was around. And she couldn't lay her eggs until everything was safe. What if nothing were ever safe?

Is it possible to root for both the wasp and the scientist? How can one be both an existentialist and an optimist? Are these questions useless? Are we like the wasp, stuck in these cycles of thought?

But in the story, I thought, *it's the scientist that causes all the trouble. The wasp just suffers.*

I couldn't help but feel that by telling me about the wasp, he was obliquely telling me something about myself, or revealing what he thought of me. The rest of the paragraph was no easier to stomach. Constant stopped writing about wasps and crickets, and turned instead to beetles.

Imagine we all have a box with something inside—say, a beetle. You can't look into anyone else's box, only your own. Everyone says they have a beetle, but you only know what a beetle is by looking into your own box. Isn't it possible that everyone has a different thing in their box? Some people might even have nothing at all—their boxes might be empty.

The beetle is Wittgenstein's, but the worry belongs to all of us. Correspondence theory tells us to measure truth by how accurately it relates to the objective world. But language is not a reflection of the objective world—only our subjective interpretation of this complicated earth. It all depends on your beetle, in your box. Language changes how we see the world, but it doesn't change the world. For us, there is only the text.

I do have a girlfriend, though right now she is not my girlfriend. You're right that words are difficult, especially those regarding our relationships with each other. Friend, of course, is too small a word for you.

At first I was thrilled. I was more than a friend to him— that was all I had wanted him to say. But it was impossible to read this without acknowledging the line above it: he did have a girlfriend, just not right now. I didn't know what that meant, but it couldn't be good news. How often was she *not* his girlfriend? It was clear that Constant didn't really want to talk about her, but then why did he bring it up in the first place, on the ferry? What did it all mean?

Despite all this, I was relieved he'd written back. I had become keenly aware of how ephemeral our entire arrangement was, how easy it would be for either of us to slip, like ghosts, from the other's life. I didn't know where Constant lived or what he did during the day. I didn't even have his phone number. At first this had seemed like a decent way to do things, even the best way; it gave our cloud conversations a certain importance. We talked about real things,

things that mattered, and didn't debase ourselves with frivolous details: our lives, our daily routines. Then those things began to matter less and less, until—I told myself—they didn't hurt so much and weren't so unbearable to live with.

I uncovered a roach infestation in the cabinet where we kept the trash. None of us was really surprised by this. We took the trash out infrequently because the dumpster outside was ringed in rat traps, and we often found dead ones in the bins. The landlord was reluctant to call us an exterminator. Finally Georgie called Harold, who assigned one of his first-year associates to the task of threatening our landlord with small claims court.

The exterminator was jolly and arrived with a tank of poison on his back. He explained the whole thing while we watched through cracks in our doors. "See, the smell tempts them out. It's irresistible—smells just like heaven to 'em. Once they're out here, the floor is lava." He guffawed at this. "Burns them right up, like that." He snapped his fingers with cheer. "And that's the end of your problem."

The roaches, like Constant's wasp, could not help themselves. I felt guilty for finding the infestation in the first place. I stared at a roach writhing between two linoleum tiles.

"It's all right," the exterminator said, catching my

expression. "Hey, now, they go real quick. Doesn't even hurt them. They're dead before they notice."

He too seemed to be talking obliquely about me.

A feeling settled over me: Constant and I were doing something we weren't supposed to be doing. None of our actions were wrong, exactly, on their own. We wrote to each other, and once in a while we took a walk together in the dark. But when I looked at the arc of the time I had known him, something seemed off.

It was harder and harder to deny that the document had an unhealthy grip on me. I discovered that in the edit history of the document I could not only read every past version, I could see words appear and disappear letter by letter, moving through time. I could see where Constant wrote whole paragraphs in a manic rush, and how sometimes he stopped for hours between sentences. In turn, he could see the sentences I wrote, deleted, and retyped again, but because I thought of him as less neurotic than me, I hoped beyond hope he didn't check the edit history. I stopped reading other things, books or the news or even most of the texts Georgie sent me.

It was easy to ignore the whole situation of the sometimes girlfriend, because I didn't understand it, and because Constant seemed to be encouraging me to do so by writing to me, and by meeting me in strange, romantic places. Lying in my bed, rereading the dense blocks of text, the parameters of right and wrong or good and bad seemed like linguistic games.

For us, there is only the text. It was almost three in the morning. I had done it—thirteen days had passed, and I could finally write back to him.

Do you remember the part in *The Little Prince* where the pilot is trying to draw the prince a sheep? The first one is too small, the second is too sickly. The pilot gets frustrated—he has to fix his plane, get out of the Sahara, return to the world. Finally he draws a crate for the little prince and says, "Here, this is just the crate. The sheep you wanted is inside." The little prince exclaims, "But this is just the one I wanted!"

Maybe this is why children are better at languages than adults. Language is so inefficient. Think about how you would explain a penalty shot to a baby. It would take hours, because before you can explain a penalty, you have to explain the concept of a goal, of boundaries, of soccer, of time, of fairness, even of games. Then it becomes obvious that even the words we use don't correspond to real, physical things, but representations of them, or even copies of those representations. What is the truth? How can we get to it?

I'm not sure what we're talking about anymore—language or existence or ourselves. I think maybe it's obstacles to understanding, which have to do with both the language and the speaker. But now we're so many metaphors deep it's hard to say if our goal is still understanding, or if it has turned to something else. What's a sheep? What's a beetle? Is this a game? If no one can look at anyone else's beetle, the word *beetle* becomes meaningless. That means words like *existentialism* or *love* or *language* aren't useful at all.

I think nothing is real, everything has already ended. I think we should stop writing to each other. But here I go typing again.

When I finished, it was two in the morning again. I tapped the clock several times, sure I was in a dream in which even clocks had stopped being useful. Obviously, I didn't understand anything, not even time. It wasn't until I woke up the next morning, and it was still dark, that I realized daylight saving must have ended.

In addition to Benny, I started tutoring another girl in the West Village, a reedy sixteen-year-old who looked older than me. She was also better than me at math and didn't seem to need a tutor at all. She kept flipping through a practice book thicker than she was and explaining problems to me.

"The E train leaves Penn Station going thirty miles an hour. Fifteen minutes later, the A train departs going fifty-five miles an hour. How long does it take the A train to overtake the E train?"

According to Zeno, eternity. By the time the A train closed the gap formed by the E train's head start, the E train would have another head start. To reach any point, first you had to get half of the way, and before that a fourth of the way, an eighth of the way, a sixteenth of a way—there were infinite steps, infinite obstacles. All motion was impossible.

The real answer had to do with determining the head-start distance and then subtracting the rates of speed. It would take the A train eighteen minutes to catch the E train. The answer was right there; she bubbled it in neatly. But I thought Zeno was also right, which was why the express train never saved you as much time as you hoped.

On Thanksgiving Day there was an uncommon warm front. Georgie convinced me to climb the service ladder to the roof—she needed someone to hand up her bong. I had never been to our roof before, because I had always assumed the upper hatch was nailed down, but apparently Georgie went up often.

"All you have to do," she panted, pushing on the hatch with her whole upper body while she clung precariously to the ladder, which clung precariously to the wall, "is push with your shoulders. . . ."

She struggled like Atlas. At last the heavy hatch budged an inch, then two, and slid loose to reveal a rectangle of clear bright sky. Georgie scrambled up and out of sight. Then she reappeared, silhouetted against all that blue. I carefully passed her bong, a custom glass creation she'd bought from a studio in Gowanus, and then started climbing after her.

It felt like the last good day. The weather was positively

balmy. Georgie unfolded a tapestry across the white bitumen. We took off our coats and basked. I watched Georgie dump the contents of her water bottle into the bong and pack her bowl. Being around her was such a sensory experience; with Georgie, everything was saturated. The colors in her bong grew more vivid in her hands, and she billowed out great clouds of white cumulus that drifted high, then dispersed. Her hair had a whole life of its own. Around her, things were more real, the opposite of Constant.

"When you smoke," I said, "does everything start feeling like a dream?"

"Oh, sure," said Georgie. "Alcohol is like borrowing happiness from the next day, but smoking is like borrowing your dreams. I think weed suppresses your REM cycle, so you're literally borrowing your dreams for waking life. Then you sleep badly. But I can't lucid dream, so it's the best I can do."

She tried to pass me her bong. I shook my head. I was thinking through my night with Constant: the infinite meadow, the talk of Sisyphus, the ferry rocking gently through the tar-black East River. All this time I'd thought the dream-state effect of the night was a quality of Constant—but how much had been the marijuana? And how was it that everyone seemed to know more about the world than I did?

Georgie's phone started to ring. It was the Harolds. She went downstairs to talk to them. While she was gone, I stretched out across the roof, which radiated warmth like a summer afternoon. From street level, the town houses on our block appeared a uniform height, but on the roof there was an entire landscape: disparate shapes all coated in the same reflective paint, chimneys and antennas, neighboring houses with skylights or proper roof decks. I stared until everything looked alien. Then I thought about Constant. I couldn't stop thinking about Constant. I noticed I felt most suspicious that I was dead whenever I wrote back to him— when I was waiting for him to respond. The dead feeling made it difficult to do simple things like wash my hair or eat vegetables. Regardless of whether I had succeeded at the water tower, Constant made me want to jump again, because it felt so difficult to be me, waiting for him to write back.

I inched along the roof until I was lying over the cornice, which jutted out over the edge of the building, so when I peeked down I saw fifty feet of empty space. I looked down until my vision tunneled.

"What are you doing?"

I jumped back, startled. Georgie had returned.

"I . . . ," I mumbled something about the view.

Georgie said nothing. Her eyes were red, but since she had smoked, it took me a moment to realize she was crying.

"What's wrong?" I asked. "What happened?"

Georgie collapsed on the blanket and made herself as

small as possible, twisting her arms around her legs and one leg around the other. She didn't say anything. I crept back from the edge and sat across from her, on the far corner of the blanket.

"Georgie?"

She sniffled and buried her head in her arms. I felt suddenly that I *was* a bad friend, worse to Tashya and Georgie than either of them were to me. Tashya would know what to say if she were here; she was good at tenderness and empathy. Georgie knew how to diffuse a situation, to pull you out of the hole you dug for yourself. But I felt useless and awkward, unable to think of a single thing to say.

"Do you mind if we skip Thanksgiving dinner at the Harolds'?" she finally said in a muffled voice.

"No," I said, surprised. "Wait, what happened? Are you okay?"

"I'm fine," she snapped. "Sorry. They're just—god, they're killing me." She rummaged around for a napkin before she gave up and blew her nose in some rolling papers. "Do you think I should go back to doing stand-up?"

Again, I didn't know what to say. Georgie was funnier than the average person, but I had never actually seen her perform a set. She wasn't afraid of people, like I was, unless they came together in a critical mass, in which case she came down with debilitating stage fright. It seemed like something that might hinder a comedy career.

"Well, I think you're really funny," I said. "What happened to the earrings?"

"No one bought any," she wailed. "Also, I hate peddling things. The market is broken and the system is shit. What's even the point of anything? God, Ocean, I don't know what to do. I hate school. I don't learn anything in a classroom, and I don't even *want* to learn anything that's going to land me an office job. Dad and Harold think the internet has rotted my mind and attention span so that I can't finish anything I start. But the internet is where I learn anything useful at all."

She dropped her head again and screamed into the arm of her coat. I jumped. A flock of birds departed from the tree across the street. Then it was so quiet for several minutes I wondered if I had gone deaf.

In a small voice, Georgie said, "Am I a mess?"

I looked at her. It had never crossed my mind that Georgie would think of herself this way. Georgie was wonderful to be around. She could make anyone laugh. Her personality was so large it made her appear taller than she really was. She was so alive it made me feel more alive just being around her. I wanted to tell her these things; I really did. But the words sounded all wrong in my head, fake even though I was sincere, somehow too much even though I meant them with all my heart.

"Why does everyone have to end up doing the same thing?" she cried. "Why does everyone have to go to college, and then spend all of their twenties at the bottom rung of some corporate ladder, and then spend all of their thirties and forties and fifties saving for retirement? Shouldn't we want more diversity of interest? Why do I have to do what everyone else is doing?"

"You don't," I said, but I wasn't even convincing myself. I was resigned to a four-year institution after my brief stint of independence; I couldn't really imagine an alternative. I was too anxious and too poor to forsake the common path as Georgie was doing, but even she was having doubts. I thought, of course, of Constant. It depressed me to think that he was right, and we weren't so different from his poor wasp, with nowhere to turn. For a safe home, we ran in a hundred circles. In order to pay rent, we had to work for causes that were mediocre or even immoral. It wasn't like I believed in the value of standardized testing, or that my tutoring was worth what Olivia and the other parents paid me. I guess this was Constant's point—that all of our choices were bad, and nonetheless we had to choose between them.

"Did the Harolds say something?" I tried.

Georgie sniffed. "They really like to forget they adopted me," she said. "Like, they can't imagine that my neurological abilities might be different from theirs, even Harold the neurosurgeon. Both Dad and Harold spent a decade in higher education. Can you imagine? Those stuffy old classrooms? They can threaten to cut me off, but I still won't move back home. I'll get a job." She glanced at me. "I'm not really cut out to tutor, though."

"Honestly," I said, thinking of Benny, "you probably are."

But Georgie wasn't listening—she was still fuming. "Parents," she said miserably, "are bad friends."

I looked at her. "What do you mean?"

She blew out a breath. "When you're little, your parents try so hard to get you to think that they're cool, and adventurous, like they're there to save you," she said. "It really goes to their heads."

I considered this. My mother wasn't really like that—and then I thought, maybe she was. All my life, my mother had gotten us out of every tight corner we had ever been backed into. I couldn't imagine how she did it. Probably if someone dropped me in a foreign country where I knew no one and had no money and barely spoke the language, I would have hurled myself off a building.

"But then your context changes," Georgie continued. "And your parents stop having relevant advice—like, you have a whole different set of problems, and there's no explaining that to them. They just want to be involved. But they're too far outside your experience, and you've made this whole new set of memories without them. But they still want to feel involved." She sighed. "I wish they would just leave me alone. I can figure this out on my own, I know I can, if they would just—fuck off. The Harolds have become really bad friends.

They used to be my best friends, even Harold the neuro-surgeon. When I was little, we used to go to the farmers' market for breakfast every Sunday, and they would let me drag them to the dog park and just sit there for hours, before we had Dostoyevsky and Pushkin." She was crying again. "Why do people have kids? It's terrible to end up with adult children, and it's even worse to be one."

She leaned into me and cried into my armpit for a long time. I held her; it felt good to hold her. For ages we just sat there, not at the edge of the roof but smack in the middle of it, until the lights of the Manhattan skyline became visible through the treetops.

Eventually I coaxed Georgie down from the roof. She smoked another bowl and promptly fell asleep. I texted Tashya to come home instead of going to the Harolds, and when she got back, we woke Georgie and spent two hundred dollars on Thai takeout. Georgie decided to suspend her veganism for the night, on account of Thanksgiving and also her emotional distress. When the food arrived, Georgie made us pass her bong around and say something we were thankful for.

"I'm thankful for my dogs, my friends, peanut sauce, and for the cow that died so I could eat it, and also for the six hundred gallons of water that probably went into this piece of meat," Georgie rattled off, and took a huge hit before she dug into her food.

Tashya took the bong gingerly. "I'm grateful we're all together," she said. "And I'm grateful I finally got into the good practice room this week."

She only took half a hit before she passed the bong to me, so I had to finish it off before I could be grateful for anything. It went straight to my head. I coughed violently, my eyes swimming.

"I'm grateful for the subway," I said, when I could. Tashya gave me a strange look. Georgie was busy eating.

We ate until we couldn't move. I had ordered duck. I thought of my mother, who was probably eating duck and thinking about me. The weed made this extraordinary to me; I couldn't stop thinking about her, and I couldn't stop eating. At some point Georgie dug out a bottle of terrible wine from the back of the fridge. Past midnight, we all passed out on the kitchen floor.

THE INFINITE Q

Again, Constant deleted my paragraphs. At first I thought he hadn't written anything in response, but then I noticed a new star on the map where there used to only be a station: Brighton Beach, on the Q line. Next to the star, Constant had written Tomorrow, 5 p.m.

Had he even read what I had written? Again I was consumed by the question. In the edit history I could see when he appeared in the document, and then, several minutes later, when he highlighted the block of text and deleted it. I looked at the time stamps for a long time, trying to determine if that was enough time for him to read my paragraphs. Everything was subtext. All subtext was bullshit.

Of course I wouldn't go meet him at Brighton Beach. I wouldn't make it, anyway—I had to tutor Benny on the Upper West Side at three. But then Olivia called to say that Benny had come down with a fever, and couldn't we please reschedule? She told me to send her my available times. I couldn't imagine what to send: my completely blank calendar? We settled on Friday afternoon. Until then I had nothing to do. I got on a train to Brighton.

The Q to the beach was almost entirely above ground. The sun hit me square in the face and I could only squint out the window as the landscape shifted: the apartment buildings grew shorter until they gave way to a patch of Victorian houses, which turned back to squat brick two-stories. In some places, the track curved so close to the buildings I could imagine diving out the train window onto a reflective roof. I marveled at the fact that all the houses were filled with people who watched dozens of trains rumble by every day.

At the last stop I got off, feeling disoriented. I couldn't say where the beach was. The platform was elevated but offered only a good view of the tall, brutalist apartment buildings on both sides. Constant wasn't there. I waited for a while, to see if he would appear. The train I'd come on pulled out of the station and headed onward without me.

At street level, I found myself in some alternate history where the Cold War had ended more favorably for the USSR. Everything still looked like New York—there were still ninety-nine-cent stores and bodegas and clothing boutiques selling variously bedazzled polyblends—but every single storefront was in Russian. An old woman shouldered past with an enormous pot of noodles, muttering in Polish.

I walked a few blocks in the wrong direction; even the street signs were in Cyrillic letters.

By the time I found the beach, the weather had changed for the worse. The wind swept off the sunlight, and the clouds blowing in were storm-dark and low. The temperature plummeted. The sea hurled itself again and again at the sand, then retreated back to the horizon. Everything was the color of cement.

Except Constant. There he was, in a neon vest, painting in the sand. He was the only person on the beach. My heart was thrumming. The wind had done something wonderful to his hair. Then I was self-conscious about my own hair, which I hadn't washed that morning and which had mostly fallen loose from sloppy braids. I had to physically resist the urge to smooth it back. Then I was angry. What right did he have to make me feel self-conscious? What right did he have to drag me around the city, after ignoring me for weeks? And why did I keep showing up—why did I care about what he had to say?

Then he raised his head and saw me. Even from a distance I could see how happy he was to see me, and that made it all worth it. He was painting the biggest subway map I had ever seen, big enough to walk right into.

"Ocean," he said when I reached him. "I wasn't sure you'd come."

Just like that I was devastated again. I shouldn't have come. And now that I was here, I knew I had to confront him. I had to ask him how he could be so happy to see me, and still have a girlfriend. I had to ask him what he thought we were doing, because I was sure it didn't match what I thought—not once had we ever come to the same conclusion.

"Are you allowed to paint on the sand like this?" I asked. "Won't it get washed out with the tide?"

"Ah, right—here." From one of his large pockets he pulled out another neon vest. I shrugged it on over my giant mustard coat. "No one will stop us in these," he said.

But isn't the paint bad for the sea? was what I meant. I wished I could make normal conversation, instead of feeling persistently anxious. I put one foot on the 7 line, then another, until I'd crossed his little Manhattan.

Constantine stood back and surveyed his work. "We have to get these onto playgrounds," he said. "Sell them to the city. Just imagine all those little kids playing tag on these—they'll never get lost again."

I focused on switching to the F line. I was afraid to look at him; I was worried by the wave of tenderness that came over me when he said that, how immediately it became the only thing I felt. In my palms I felt a pulse of physical attraction—for his hands clasped behind his back, for his tousled black hair—as he paced the A line across Brooklyn. He looked just like a philosopher, I thought.

He glanced at me. "You're so quiet."

I was always quiet. Constant did most of our talking. It

was easier to write to him, easier to think of things to say when we weren't face-to-face. I shrugged and fidgeted with my hands. At Utica Avenue he sat back on his heels and looked at me, his coat puddling on the surrounding stations. I was venturing into Queens. There was no transfer between us; we could never reach each other, only run parallel, several miles apart.

"Why did you say you would stop writing?" he asked suddenly.

Why couldn't I ask him my questions so easily? Why should I be so anxious to say these things to him, when it was clear he wasn't anxious at all?

"Why did you write to me in the first place?" I asked. "In the subway that night, why did you come across the tracks?"

I could hear the dread in my own voice. He was going to say that he'd had too much time on his hands, or that it had started as a joke. I felt, in my sternum, that he was going to laugh at me for asking.

But he didn't. He propped his chin on his hand and looked at me for several long moments. I often had a hard time maintaining eye contact without feeling embarrassed, but Constant had no such issue.

"When I saw you," he said eventually, "I felt like I already knew you. I mean, I felt so sure we were going to know each other, which is almost the same thing as already being friends. I had things to tell you. Does that make sense? Then

I had that dream, and I thought you would know what it meant for sure."

I peered at him carefully, to see if he meant it. I tried not to let the thrill that went through me when he said that show on my face. Then I remembered that we *hadn't* thought his dream meant the same thing, and I was confused. But Constant plowed on.

"When you wrote to me about language, I understood you," he said.

It felt so good to hear that: *I understood you.*

He kept going. "Language is . . . *atomic*. The whole weave of our reality is atoms latching on to or repelling each other, and all of it is random. Accidental. And somehow it makes up everything. Language is like that too. With the same elementary alphabet, you can make both tragedies and comedies. That's what Democritus said. You can make truth or absurdity. Doesn't it seem impossible that anyone can say anything? You're right—when we talk to people, we might be having entirely different conversations. But when I talk to you, I don't think about those things. We can just . . . talk."

I *did* think about those things, I thought. When I wrote to him that language felt hellish to me, I was trying to say that our conversations made me feel worse, not better. But Constant had only responded saying that *language* was the problem, not our dubious relationship. I had stopped on Mets-Willets Point. If we both reached out, our fingertips would touch. But inside the map, on our own lines, I felt miles and miles away from him. I didn't say anything.

"If you stopped writing," said Constant, "I would miss you."

The feeling in my chest was so physical I almost doubled over.

"I would keep writing," he continued, "and hope you found it someday. I would always keep writing to you."

It felt like he was punching me over and over. I never wanted him to stop talking. We were both quiet for a long time.

"I'd be sorry if you stopped writing back," said Constant. He said it very seriously. There was a dark green tone to his coat that made his eyes piercing. I was ridiculous with feeling. "I would have been sorry if you didn't come today. I wasn't sure if you would. I wasn't sure you'd see the map in time."

"I'm here," I said. The lump in my throat made my own voice unrecognizable to me.

"Yeah," Constant said. He held out a hand and dragged me to him. "I saw you shivering when you were still all the way down the beach, even though your coat is the biggest one I've ever seen. Come on, let's get you a drink."

On the boardwalk, there were three restaurants, two of which were called Tatiana.

"It burns down every few years," said Constant as we passed the first Tatiana on our way across the boardwalk. "It burned the same day Notre Dame was burning. What's funny is when they first built two Tatianas, they asked the owner, whose name is Tatyana, 'Why two?' And she said, 'In case of fire!'"

Inside, we were the only patrons. The decor was consistent with the early eighties. Constant, who had clearly been there before, led me to the bar, where an enormous man was smoking long cigarettes and paying us no attention. He was almost as tall as Constant, which was disorienting, as though the restaurant changed the scale of things.

"Constantine," I whispered.

"Yeah," he said. "What is it?"

"I don't have my fake," I said.

"Your fake?" he said. He didn't lower his voice; I glanced at the bartender.

"My fake ID," I mumbled.

"Oh," said Constant, "you're not twenty-one." He said it thoughtfully, like it hadn't occurred to him. "Well, I think that's fine. I mean, I don't think it matters. It's not really that sort of establishment. Look, we even choose our own glasses."

He took me to a decrepit white refrigerator in the corner, which I hadn't noticed until then. Inside it was full of cold, dusty beer steins and shot glasses. Constant handed me a glass with either a bear or a monkey emblazoned on it in chipped paint; the glass read CHEBURASHKA. His had an alligator and read GENA. I followed Constant back to the bartender. Both of them stared at me.

"You have to give him your glass," said Constant.

I did.

"Now you have to pick a vodka," Constant explained. There was laughter in his voice. I pointed at the bottle closest to me, wanting the ordeal to be over. It turned out to be gin. Constant took over, grinning. I followed him to a table, feeling like he had handed me another Sisyphean task.

"Drink this," he said, handing me the shot. "It will make you warm."

As we sat, he started telling me about a painting he had fallen in love with. He didn't use the word *love*; it was much worse than that. He talked about the painting in terms of the philosopher Martin Buber. Buber wrote that there were only two sorts of relationships. The I-It relationship was the common relationship, the one of practical necessity; it was the language we used to order coffee or ask for directions, without fully engaging or acknowledging the humanity of another person, the relationship we had with our bartenders or coworkers or even most of our friends. I glanced at the bartender when Constant said that, worried he would overhear. Then there was the I-You relationship—the relationship in which you could fully be with a person, or even an animal or a tree or a piece of art, without miscommunication, just existing together in the spontaneous present. He really said those words: *without miscommunication*. I couldn't believe it. Did he really think it was easier to communicate with a painting than with me?

"I was standing in front of this painting," Constant said. "It felt just like writing to you, like I was perfectly aligned with the intention of the artist, like we were both there in that moment as it unfolded."

"Constantine," I blurted, because I couldn't stand it anymore, "we don't know anything about each other."

He was surprised. "Of course we do," he said.

But it was so obvious we didn't. How could he say these things to me, if he knew anything about me? Did he mean he was in love with me—that understanding someone was the same as loving them? But he didn't understand me, I thought, dejected. That was the whole problem.

He saw my face and became serious. "Ocean," he said. "You can ask me anything you want. You can always ask me."

I nodded. I took a sip of vodka. It didn't make me warm, only nauseous. My heart was pounding, and my cheeks were red.

"How old are you?" I asked him.

"Twenty-one," he said. "Well, twenty-two next month."

I choked. *Twenty-two?* That was older than I could even imagine: twenty-two was another life. Even Tashya was only twenty-one, and that was already so far outside my experience

I had no real concept of her life or her worries.

"I'm graduating in May," he said, "and then it's grad school. But now I want to defer a year, like you. Bum around in Colorado and ski, maybe, or hike."

I was worried the alcohol was making me sick. I didn't want to ask any more questions. I didn't know what to do with these answers, which seemed to make everything worse. I felt intimidated that he was so much older than me; I hated feeling young, four years shorter in experience. But beneath my belly I felt something else, incongruent—a tug toward him. *Twenty-two*, I kept thinking, *twenty-two*. I looked at the monkey or the bear on my glass, then the crocodile on his.

"And your girlfriend," I finally said.

"Ah," he said. "Yes, that." He looked at his glass, and then threw his head back and drank it all at once. "Her name is Adeline. She's abroad."

"Abroad?" *Adeline,* I thought. Adeline and Constantine. They fit together so well, rounding out each other's consonants.

"In Prague," he said. "For the semester. She's studying art history. We haven't spoken since she left. We agreed not to. So she could have the . . ." He waved a hand. "Abroad experience, you know. Anyway, she's not allowed to speak English while she's there, and I can't speak Czech, so . . ."

"The semester is nearly over," I said.

"Yes," said Constant. He was frowning. He was quiet for

so long I became agitated. I didn't know what to do, so I copied him and took a drink too.

"What do you mean, the abroad experience?" I said.

Constant was wry. "I think it means, able to act on the European erotic imagination."

I considered what that meant. "Like, she's hooking up with other people?"

I watched his face carefully. He didn't look upset, exactly, or even jealous—he looked more amused than anything. "Well," he said, "we're not exclusive. The I-You relationship should be an open and dynamic one. We don't doubt that our friends like us just because they have other friends. But we expect romance to be jealous. You know what I mean?"

I didn't know what anything meant. I felt resigned and devastated. So Constantine loved this girlfriend, even though she was only sometimes his girlfriend. I felt like I was wading into the deep end of the pool and could hardly keep my head above the water. It seemed like overnight everyone except me had become an adult. Tashya and Georgie argued like they were married, and all of Georgie's friends seemed so experienced with their sexuality it had become background in their lives, something necessary but ordinary. And here was Constant, in some kind of radical relationship. I hadn't even kissed anyone since a seventh-grade game of truth or dare, which probably didn't count.

"What are you thinking about?" Constant asked.

I sighed. "Growing pains."

He was amused. "Yeah?"

"I was thinking, when you're growing physically, you can point to your joints and say, look, the pain is here, and someone will tell you it's okay, that it's normal. Your bones stop stretching outward, but the pain doesn't stop. It just changes."

I couldn't explain anymore. I had a hollow, unfriendly feeling in my chest. And the pain went on, in places I couldn't point to, in a way that I knew didn't correspond to my physical well-being. The world was changing too quickly; before I could adapt to my last environment, everything shifted again. I had read once that the cognitive revolution had made humans good at making social changes faster than other animals—but if that was true, what was wrong with me? Why was I so slow?

Eventually Constant had to finish my shot. He reassured me it wasn't a good vodka, but he threw it back with ease. I watched his throat move and felt desire in the palms of my hands. He put the glass down and looked at me. I was so embarrassed I wanted to stick my head in the fridge.

"What now?" I asked.

Constant smiled. "My god, Ocean. Only life."

We walked toward Coney Island. The lights on all the rides were off, and the colors were garish. What few carnival workers had to be there were dressed in pinstripes and dismal with boredom. The vodka had made me suddenly, nightmarishly tired. I wished I hadn't come to meet Constant in the freezing cold, to listen to him talk about love and his girlfriend. Nonetheless, when I realized that we were heading toward the train, where he would eventually leave me, I dragged my feet.

We walked slowly, kicking at shells with our heels. Nearly all of them were finely broken, so we trudged on a mosaic of exoskeleton, burying them farther into the sand. It had started to rain, but so delicately that for a while it felt like we were just wading through thick fog, until all of a sudden we were soaked. The ocean came close, then retreated. The sand found its way into my boots, and then even my socks.

Constant stopped and bent down. "Here," he said. "Sea glass."

He dropped it in my palm. It wasn't old; the edges were barely worn. It was the exact same blue as the night sky of the power outage: electric, unearthly. I squinted at it, then held it up.

"It's the same color," I said, amazed. "Like, exactly."

"Plucked from memory," he said. Like he had conjured it. I couldn't stop staring at it, or marveling at how just holding it seemed to solidify my memory and perception of everything—the first night in the subway tunnels and the strange night on the ferry and today at Brighton, and all of the things we had written to each other along the trajectory. The jagged sliver of glass seemed heavier than it was, like an anchor.

Before I could stop myself, I put my palm on his chest. It was solid and harder than I expected, even beneath his layers. There he was, as real as I was. Then I saw my hand, on his body, and was horrified. Before I could snatch it back, he caught it in his. The despair I felt was pitiful, infinite. All I wanted was to pause time, to prevent the future from happening. Suddenly I understood what Constant had been trying to tell me all along—that the present was preferable to the past, which was unforgiving, or the future, which was relentless. And we were both here, and the moment was passing. There it was again, the panic that made it difficult to be alive. I was tired of feeling things, especially this. I wasn't allowed to opt out of living, of earning money or going to school. Instead I had to trudge on, like paddling forever against a riptide, pretending I wasn't already lost at sea. Every time he left me, it got worse. How could I explain this to Constant? How many times would he let me try, before he understood what I felt? *Only life.* That was the very problem.

I already knew what would happen next. It was difficult to say whose fault it was. I leaned toward him, of course, but it would have been impossible to reach him if he hadn't leaned down. He kissed me. I could hardly feel my face, but I could still taste the sharp bitterness on his lips, the vodka that I couldn't seem to get away from. The wind tousled our hair. When Constantine kissed me it felt just like being on the water tower. It blew every other thought out of my mind, like I had evaporated.

When it was over, I was both relieved and devastated. Constant, still leaning over me, smiled. He took a loose strand of my hair and tugged, gently, at the end. "Let's get out of here," he said. And I followed him off the pier, dazed, tingling, so cold I couldn't feel my toes.

IN THE BLACK-AND-WHITE ROOM

Then it was time to go home for Christmas. Tashya left first, because she had a concert after the break and wanted to go home to her own piano. Then Georgie went uptown because she missed the dogs. For a few blurry days, it was only me in the apartment. A disturbing quiet settled. I became so anxious I had to stop several times a day to catch my breath. I was only going home for a week—I'd told my mother that I had to be back early for a January-term class—but the thought of seeing my mother at the airport and lying to her for a hundred and sixty-eight hours straight was making me dizzy with fear. I couldn't stop thinking of all the things that could go wrong, how I could slip up, and how she would find out everything, and refuse to let me return; then I would be stuck, dead, under the shadow of the beckoning water tower.

It took me all day to pack. I kept getting exhausted, and had to take several breaks, invariably ending up on the untitled document. There were no updates from Constant.

But since he had arranged the outing to Brighton, maybe it was my turn to write. It was hard to be sure. It was hard to be sure of anything; nothing was defined.

I felt more unmoored than ever. Slowly the city emptied out.

On the plane, I paid for Wi-Fi so I could check the document. It was still blank, and I felt stupid for paying for an hour of internet. Georgie had texted several pictures of the dogs, who looked even more comical on my small screen: mountainous Dostoyevsky, puny Pushkin. I went back to the document. I decided I had to write something, since I had already paid to do so.

In Chinese, colors are delineated differently than they are in English. There's no indigo between blue and violet, but instead another color, called qing, between green and blue. You could translate it as teal or turquoise, but it wouldn't quite be true. In fact indigo is better, because it shares this quality in hue; you see, both qing and indigo imply some deeper tinge that comes from depth. A lake, for example, can be qing or indigo, but not a puddle. The sea glass you gave me is qing, and so was the sky the night we met. I've never told anyone about the sky that night, because I don't know how to talk about it English. There are even words missing for colors, which you'd think are pretty elementary. Of course I'm not really worried about the colors; I'm worried that I see a different world than everyone else. I'm worried that these problems of language—these gaps that get revealed when you lay two languages on top of each other—I'm worried these are the root of all my other problems in life, why often I just don't know what to say, why so much of my reality seems to exist just in my head. As you say, there is nothing but the text. The problem is fundamental.

After that, qing began to appear everywhere. Outside the round little window of the airplane, Lake Michigan was qing. The pack of biscuits the flight attendant handed out came in a qing package. The trash bag she later came around with was qing. Exiting the plane, I saw a nurse in qing scrubs. And when I reached the curb, my mother was wearing jade earrings. Jade is the purest expression of qing.

I was already nauseous with nerves, but then, as I got closer, she looked so happy I wanted to cry. She looked really good, I thought, confirming the idea that for all parents who dreaded their empty nests, the best of their lives didn't begin until their children moved out of them.

"You're too skinny!" was the first thing she said to me, already fussing over the state of my hair and the fit of my clothes. She, on the other hand, seemed to have gained weight in all the right places. In California, said my mother, she had done nothing but eat: Korean bulgogi and hot pot and vast dim sum spreads. She'd gotten the jade earrings in California too. She'd gotten me a bracelet that matched.

She talked and talked. It wasn't until we were in the

car, halfway through the forty-minute drive home, that she started to ask about college.

"They were okay," I said, when she asked about exams. I repeated some variation of this lie when she asked about my friends, my dorm room, my professors, my TAs, my RAs, my clubs, my roommates.

"Actually," I said, "my roommates are really great."

"You seem so tired," she kept saying. "Are you getting enough sleep? Are you eating? Are you drinking water?"

By the time we pulled into the driveway I was getting a migraine from exhaustion, a sour pounding behind my left eye, soft like rot. My mother sent me straight to bed. She seemed a little disappointed to do so, like we might stay up and raid the fridge, which we had done once in a while when I was much, much younger. I was too relieved to care.

In my childhood bedroom I dropped my bags and sank into my bed and felt it in my bones: the last months had been imaginary. I pressed the heels of my hands into my eyes. It was a fever dream. It was too good and strange and painful to be true, all at the same time.

I dug around my pocket for the sea glass. For hours, I lay there just staring at it, my migraine growing steadily worse.

By morning, Constant had responded. My migraine had not obliged to dissolve itself. It persisted behind my eye, throbbing on my optic nerve. Sometimes my migraines went away after I slept, but often they lingered and came again more furiously in the morning, angry that I tried to outsmart them. It made it difficult to look at my screen, at the tiny individual words backlit in blue light.

My mother had already left for work, so I walked downstairs in the same clothes I'd worn the day before. There was a cup of coffee left in the pot, so I microwaved it and sipped drearily.

Imagine you've spent your whole life in a black-and-white room, studying color. Your language point is interesting—so let's say you speak all the languages, and have access to all the quantitative information on color across such barriers. You learn the exact wavelength combinations that must come from the sky and refract off the sea, and the physical information that the neurophysiology of the brain interprets from the rods and cones, which it then directs to the expulsion of air from the lungs, the contraction of the vocal cords, the undulations of the tongue and lips in order to say, "The ocean is blue." And then, after you've learned all there is possibly to know about color, you go outside. You see that the ocean, indeed, is blue. Have you learned anything new? Or did you already know it? Is the sensation of color more than its physical properties?

This is to say that what is meaningful about color does not reside in language—that some essential quality, as the route is essential to the train, exists only in experience. It evades us; you try to describe this color to me, but all you can really do is circle around it, approximate closer and closer, but it is obvious that it still means something more to you than it does to me. Almost everything is a beetle. Whereof one cannot speak, one must remain silent.

I read what he had written several times. It was hard not to take his thought experiment personally. With each reading it seemed more like he was saying that what I had written was useless and meaningless. Why couldn't Constant write to me about Brighton Beach, or the ferry, or the subway? Why did he act like our waking lives and our written ones were mutually exclusive—like we had nothing to do with each other?

In a fit of temper, I exited the document and just sat there, trying to drink my horrible coffee. *Whereof one cannot speak, one must remain silent.* What did that even mean? How could he say things like that to me, and also say that he would miss me if I stopped writing? What did he miss, if he thought my writing was bullshit? My migraine grew worse and worse. Eventually I had to close my eyes, though the caffeine and my frustration made it impossible to sleep. Every system was broken, nothing in the world felt good. This was clearest to me at home, where all my most dire feelings returned like water into a well.

Hours later, my mother came home and found me asleep on the table. The kitchen was now bluish and dark—it had snowed, and the white film on the ground outside turned the walls indigo. My head was still throbbing. I had hoped it would be manageable by the time my mother came back so that I could act normal enough to fool her. If she threatened me with a doctor's visit right now, I couldn't bear it, I just couldn't.

"What's wrong?" she asked immediately. She turned the lights on; my head exploded.

"Nothing," I said, garbled.

"Why were you sitting around in the dark?"

I struggled for words. "Maybe I'm jet-lagged?"

She made an impatient noise. "There's only a one-hour time difference between us."

I mumbled something about getting sick on the plane. This was a mistake. My mother disappeared into the pantry and came back with one of her herbal Chinese medicines. She steeped it in hot water and made me gulp it down. It tasted exactly as sharp as the vodka I'd had at Brighton, and it made me miss Constant so fiercely that when my mother saw my pained expression, she sent me to bed.

In bed, I watched the last light fade, draining away what little color remained. I felt physically ill. Maybe Constant was right, and all my life had been colorless.

When I woke up again, it was four in the morning and the migraine remained like an infection. It was remarkably dark in my room, a sort of dark that did not exist in the city, only here. When I put my hand in front of my nose, I couldn't even see the shape of my fingers.

I knew I had to respond to Constant, or I'd never be able to fall back asleep. But when I opened up the document and read what he'd written again, he sounded so callous, and he was so far away. Then I could only conjure up memories of him leaving me at train stations, the distinctive way his long coat flapped behind him, the way the subway doors seemed to barricade us from each other.

It was so dark I lost all sense of myself, except for the pain. In the dark, I had lost the ability to distinguish the physical boundaries of my body, the shape of me, where I ended and began. The migraine became everything; it was the only essential part of me. I could feel the shape of it, a swelling of the left half of my head, pulsing and red. Whenever my awareness went to touch the edges, it was at once repelled and inflamed by my attention. And there was an equal pain in my sternum, a rawness in my lungs, making it hard to breathe when I thought about Constant. Did he write to his girlfriend like this? Was he more careful, somehow kinder, when he spoke to her? The idea that he might have two documents, only one of them untitled, almost made me vomit.

Eventually I put my phone away and lay there in the dark until morning. The light crept in, and my mother followed. She peeked her head through the door and hovered there, just watching. I tried to keep my breathing even; I didn't want to talk to her. She stayed for a long time. I couldn't tell what she was thinking. I knew she couldn't tell what I was thinking either, and after she left I thought about that for a long time—how Constant was actually right, and no matter how many languages you knew, none of them could lift us out of our own separate bodies. It couldn't help us understand.

In the morning, he had added a paragraph.

Where are you? Have you gone home for Christmas? I accidentally found myself in Rockefeller Center yesterday, which ruined my mood. The prevailing mythology of the city at Christmastime must be the worst lie capitalism ever told. Both the marketing and the tourists make me feel like life is not worth living ("like flies on a dead thing" et al.). There is so much I want to tell you.

I had taken too long to respond; he didn't delete his own paragraph, just added more beneath it. I found myself over-thinking this, nursing another cup of microwaved coffee. Was he too anxious that I didn't read what he wrote? But I always read what he wrote and responded to it; he was the one prone to pulling new topics out of nowhere. I got more and more angry. Why did he even want me to respond, after he had told me to stay silent?

I was angry at myself too, for being so far away, and for missing him. Around Constant I felt stupid for so many reasons. And nonetheless I missed him so much there was physical pressure against my chest.

Constant talked a lot about rationality and science—was that why I felt *less* rational around him, less capable of making decisions? At Brighton, when I asked him what he would do if I stopped writing, I had been elated when he said he would miss me. But it occurred to me now that what I had wanted him to say was that he would look for me, that he would worry, that he would ask what went wrong.

Did he know, as well as I did, that I couldn't stop writing? That if he wrote and wrote and missed me, eventually, inevitably, I would write back?

Pain is one of your words without meaning. I can only feel pain in my body, and you can only feel pain in yours. Pain is a beetle in our box. We have some vocabulary: I can point at a wound and say "Ow!" or I can go to the doctor and describe a sensation as sharp or shooting or burning. But none of these are very meaningful. Once I read in an essay by Leslie Jamison that when seeking out a doctor for pain, women are more likely to be prescribed sedatives, while men are more likely to be prescribed medication. That means even *pain* means something different depending on who describes it: a man says *ow* and the doctor finds the problem, a woman says *ow* and the doctor says maybe you're exaggerating. If *pain*, the word, doesn't have meaning, its side effects do, and the side effects are unevenly distributed; somehow there is less miscommunication when men proclaim their pain than when women do. Actually, scientists think women are better at pain. Because of things like childbirth and menstruation, women have to be more sensitive to pain in order to sort out which kinds of pain are biological, and which are pathological.

You and I, we're worried everything is imaginary. It's all in our heads. If everything is in our heads, then nothing has meaning; the trouble is, our heads have to interact with each other, in extraordinary numbers, in cities of millions, in a global network of billions. And so we have to find a way to get through to each other. Language isn't perfect; it's not even that good. I tell you I'm in pain. You say it's all imaginary. I tell you I think I'm in hell. You say, Aren't we all?

I'm worried I'm falling in love with you, and that this is what you want. I can't define *love* or *think* or even *I* in any meaningful way because I don't feel like myself anymore. I'm like the train in your dream, but I can't say what is essential. Nothing is anchoring me except, sometimes, these letters. I don't know what that means; I don't know how we got here. If there are things you want to tell me, why can't you just tell me? Plainly, and not in thought experiments or metaphors or dreams or riddles? Surely there are greater lies that capitalism has told? Why are you so angry at the tourists? Is it because you've had some sort of miscommunication about Christmas?

All morning I watched two men cut down a tree in our neighbor's yard. It seemed like the wrong season for such activities. The tree was enormous; they had to prune the thinnest branches, then lop off all the higher wings, dismantling it piece by piece. Hours later, at last, they took the chain saw to the trunk. I was really worried about the squirrels. I hoped none were hibernating in the tree, or I hoped they had roused themselves long enough to escape to another yard. How dismal to be a squirrel, bothering no one, sleeping soundly, and then one day your house is felled in the most difficult season. Possibly it was even worse to be a squirrel than a wasp. Possibly it was even worse to be a tree than a squirrel.

With a final pass of the chain saw, the trunk groaned and tilted toward the ground. Falling and falling. It took an eternity before it collapsed into the snow. It was hard to say what was essential about the tree: the roots, probably, some aspect of the trunk. It was difficult to say what made a thing a thing, but it was easy to see when it ceased to be itself. Now the tree was no longer a tree. The tree service cleaned up the remains and left.

I went to the water tower. My mother had taken her new car to work, but I found the keys to the junky old one still in the drawer by the garage. By some miracle the car started, though it was more than a decade old and no one had touched it since I'd left for New York.

I wasn't sure I should be driving. I had a heady feeling

like I was waterlogged, not like I couldn't see my surroundings but like they didn't quite make sense to me. I knew both that it was a bad idea to go to the tower and that I would never be able to stop myself, that it was the thing that called me home. I ran a stop sign but only realized it much later. The water tower came into view, diminutive at a distance, too short a fall to send anything to hell. Then it rose and rose. By the time I parked beneath it, it seemed to have grown from the ground like a beanstalk. I got out of the car. The wind was dismal. The snow crunched beneath my feet, leaving behind telltale footprints in a crust of ice.

Something had changed. Where before the ladder had extended to the ground, now the bottom dozen feet or so had been removed, so that to reach the ladder you would need to come prepared with your own self-sufficient ladder. Seeing it filled me with misgiving: had they removed the bottom part as a precaution because I had fallen to my death here several months ago? There was no way to reach the bottom rung. I stared at it until my neck hurt. Had the water tower always been the same shade of blue? Hadn't it been lighter, closer to qing than indigo? Nothing was as I'd left it. All my memory was faulty.

I crouched with my back against the base of the tower. Months of cold leeched from the metal into my back; even my fat yellow coat might as well have been paper. I shivered for a while, and then began going numb, piece by piece, fingers and toes and the nape of my neck. I strained my head upward, where the bulb of the water tower stuck out from the ground like a pin in a map. *A location of importance,* I thought vaguely. I kicked at the snow on the ground.

I could never see Constant again. I had told him I loved him, which meant I had ruined my own life. I couldn't face him ever again. I wondered what the rest of his life would look like: if he would marry the sometimes girlfriend and make her a sometimes wife, if he would go on to write papers about nihilism and the universe that lots of people would read and became enchanted by, if he would sell his map to a big company that forced the MTA to make itself better. I wondered if indeed he would keep writing to me, though of course I couldn't be seen on the document again, which meant I could never check.

I buried my head in my arms. I had climbed the water tower that day last summer to make things simple, but everything had grown exponentially more complicated. I felt full of a pain that eluded me—whenever I tried to focus on it, it slipped away like oil on water. It was increasingly difficult to be in my body. The only person likely to understand was Constant, who seemed able to fill in the gaps where language failed me. But all Constant wanted to talk about were the gaps, how they nullified everything else that could possibly matter. So who was there to talk to? What was the point of talking? It was abundantly clear to me all my options were gone. I had waited too long. I couldn't even climb the water tower to try again.

I sat there for hours, until the snow soaked through my winter boots and my pants. The skin on the back of my thighs tingled with pinpricks. The clouds weren't moving; it was like time had stopped. If Constant had been here, he would tell me something about time, like why it was slower in the mountains than at sea. If Constant were here, he would have figured out a way to reach the bottom rung, and then he too would want to climb. I knew that he felt the same thrill I did at the edge of nothing. He too liked to peer into the dark.

I was shivering so hard my vision had doubled. What was going to happen next? What was I hurtling toward, and how would I deal with it? Again I looked up to see the bulbous top of the tower, so high above. What a long fall. The world looked so different at the base than from the top; they might have been two worlds altogether. My migraine had frozen but was still weighing behind my eye, lopsided. All I wanted was to check the document again, but I was sure my heart would rupture to see what I had written. *I'm worried I'm falling in love with you.* What had possessed me to write that, to tell him, in a document that tracked my every keystroke, in a language I couldn't retract?

I sat there for as long as I could, until the sky again drained itself and the dark took over. I had known there would be no answers here, but I felt crushed anyway. There,

above me, was the place I had fainted, or jumped. Forward or
back. Life was full of contradictions. Was the real purgatory
never knowing anything at all?

I drove home. The heat trickled out wetly at first and
then five minutes later turned blistering. When I got home I
was soaking wet and so cold I made myself scan for signs of
frostbite, which was difficult with my wooden fingers. I took
off my wet clothes and went to sit in the downstairs bathroom, where the tiles were always warm from the furnace.
The bathroom was a shade of teal or turquoise, but not qing.
I climbed into the bathtub and lay there, fetal. I felt like I
was losing my mind.

I woke up pierced by light. My mother was standing over me.

"Ocean," she said. "Sun Haiying," she actually said.
"What's the matter with you?"

My whole body seemed to seize, like she had struck me
with a tuning fork. *What's the matter with you?* It was less
harsh in Chinese, but it still made me want to hold myself
safely behind my ribs. "Let me be!" my whole being was
screaming.

"Tell me what's wrong," she said. Her voice had risen in
pitch, begging.

I couldn't look at my mother. I could feel her panic, but
I couldn't think of what to say to reassure her. I couldn't tell
her again that I was depressed, because I couldn't explain it.

Nothing was really wrong with me; nothing had ever happened to me. There was no trauma I could point at, but I felt drained all the time, dried out like a husk. I couldn't even get myself out of the tub; I couldn't think of a single motivating reason. It was warm here, and my body fit right into the curve of the ceramic. I wished she would just turn off the lights and leave.

My mother came into the bathroom and drew me physically up, her fingers digging into my upper arm. She shook me once, hard. "How did you get like this?" she asked. "What happened to you?"

None of it was right in English. In Chinese, and in the way she said it, she was more desperate than accusing. Nonetheless I translated her words badly, and absorbed them like blows. I shook her off and stepped out of the tub. My migraine had become suddenly so much worse I could hardly see, and my vision filled with alternating bright bursts and dark spots. I was crying, but more because of the migraine than my mother. I wanted to know how I got like this too.

"My head really hurts," I managed. "I just need to lie down. I'm really sorry."

Our eyes met briefly. I look very little like my mother except in the eyes, where we had the same hooded inner corners, the same sparse eyelashes. I realized in that moment that my mother had an entirely different set of memories of me than I did of myself, that probably she had memories of me where I was not perpetually depressed, whereas I had none. I didn't know which was worse. I really was sorry. I left her in the bathroom and collapsed in my dark, quiet room.

For the rest of the week, we said almost nothing, but my mother made all of my favorite food: wood-ear mushroom dumplings, char siu pork belly, braised short ribs with wide rice noodles. The migraine grew steadily worse, until on Christmas Day I was so nauseous I had to make some excuse after dinner to go retch quietly in my bathroom. There was nothing to be done. There was no language between us; there was only food. My mother had to make it, so I knew she loved me. I had to eat it, so she knew I loved her. Every night, she sliced me another plate of fruit.

The day before I was set to fly back to the city, I checked the untitled document. I had nothing left to lose. Constant had responded. Immediately I exited the document. My pounding heart made my migraine feel like someone was taking jackhammers to my brainstem and my left eyeball. I opened the document. There was a paragraph, and beneath it, there were two more lines, in conspicuously diminutive text. He had chosen a much smaller font size than we had been using before and applied no capital letters. I read those lines first: an address above Central Park. Beneath it, he wrote, Find me when you're back. On the map, he had starred the closest station.

Then he had written about lobsters. Mostly he summarized David Foster Wallace's "Consider the Lobster," which I had read but which he seemed to assume I'd never heard of.

On the question of pain, it seems clear that we try to avoid it. Because you're right that pain is a totally subjective mental experience, our interaction with someone (or something) in pain comes down to two things. The first is the subject's ability to feel pain—to have the right neurological equipment, nociceptors, prostaglandins, neuronal opioid receptors, and so on. This is the lobster's problem: its nervous system isn't centralized, like ours is. What's it like to be a lobster, a wasp, a bat? How does it feel? The other is how they behave in pain—screaming and writhing and such. Language belongs to the second category: pain behavior includes these things we say, ow, burning, sharp, and so on. Without it, and as we travel further away from the ability to support it, to lobsters and wasps and bats, it becomes easier and easier to shed faith that lobsters and wasps and bats experience anything at all.

Part of avoiding pain is avoiding painful thoughts—it is much easier to think that no one and nothing else feels pain as you do. This is why we have such trouble with love.

I stared. My temper spiked. Before I could change my mind, I highlighted his paragraph and deleted it in a stroke. Constant wasn't interested in what I had to say, just in having a smarter response. He was telling me I was wrong, in such a complicated and convoluted way that I couldn't exactly point to where he did it, could accuse him of nothing, couldn't trust my own mind. He was saying, very politely, that he didn't want to talk about painful things, even if I was feeling them.

I sat back and stared at the document. I stared at the corner that said UNTITLED DOCUMENT and felt something almost like wonder that this nameless, empty thing had dismantled me.

I closed the document and turned off my computer. Then it was just me and my migraine in the dark. The rest of the world stopped existing, briefly.

WAKING LIFE

My migraine dissipated as soon as the plane approached New York City. Like a fever, it broke all at once; I blinked a few times, and my head was clear. Outside the window, Brooklyn passed beneath us, then lower Manhattan. I could see the shape of the whole island, only the size of Constant's map. The map wasn't the territory, I thought—but all at once it was incredible to me that we could have maps at all.

For the whole flight back, I had done nothing but stare at Constant's map, at the star near Hamilton Heights, at the address written beneath it. I was alternately full of conviction that I could stay away and sure I would die if I didn't go. The curiosity alone would kill me—what did he want to tell me? What else did we have to say to each other? I wasn't sure I could stand another bout of drinking or smoking; but at the same time, I would give anything, all my pride and all my dignity, to see him.

I couldn't believe I really felt this way. When I tried to think of all the things I liked about him, they evaded me.

It wasn't quite true that I liked that he was smart, because smart wasn't exactly the right word—nor thoughtful, nor intuitive, nor intelligent. I thought Constant was brilliant, and most of the time I didn't even care that he thought he was brilliant too. I liked his strange cheer, underlaid with nihilism. I liked his crooked grin beneath his crooked nose. I liked the way he had tugged at the end of my hair after he kissed me. I liked how he extended a hand to me in the dark.

Since I had only my backpack, it didn't take me long to get out of the airport. I headed for the train.

To get to the train, I had to first board a bus, where there was nowhere to sit. A volatile turn sent me flying onto the lap of a disgruntled TSA employee. It took me several stops to realize I was on the wrong bus. After I got off and crossed the street to the right bus stop, I sat there for half an hour, surveying Queens, which looked both entirely like the rest of New York and altogether different. Nothing grew here, either. All the grass was dead.

At last the bus came. It took a long time to even pass the airport again, and over an hour before we were at last crossing into Manhattan. *I should just take the train back to Brooklyn,* I thought. It didn't make sense to go to Constant; even imagining his face was unbearable. When the bus stopped at Malcolm X Boulevard, I went to the uptown subway platform and loathed myself for doing so. The distance between us felt charged. I was worried I would puke in one of the subway trash cans, which I was scared to even look into, since they often seemed to be on fire.

If I could tell my mother, I thought, she would frown and become agitated, and say I should stay away from anyone who made me feel such a thing. I couldn't think about my mother. When I'd kissed her goodbye at the airport, the way her face crumpled made me want to kill myself all over again. *My poor mother,* I thought—what had she ever done to be saddled with me?

Anyway, hadn't I been prepared all my life for such heart-sickness? Why else was the common curriculum so full of unrequited, miserable love? Wasn't Gatsby terrible to Daisy? Didn't Daisy accommodate this? Anna Karenina didn't throw herself in front of a train because both the men in her life were *good* to her, but because they loved her. Emma Bovary ruined her own life for such notions. There was something deeply unsympathetic about Daisy and Anna and Emma; the discourse always came down to that—whether or not they were *likable.*

I walked the remaining blocks to the address Constant had given me. The building was formidably enormous and spanned the whole block. What if he had changed his mind, and didn't want to see me after all? What if the girlfriend was back from Europe? What if she came to the door? I should just take the subway back to Brooklyn.

Finally I pushed the number for his apartment. Several minutes passed. *Maybe he's not even there,* I hoped. I checked the time on my phone and told myself I would leave in three minutes. I could just go home, and torture myself over the document and the meanings of words without facing any of the consequences.

Then the door opened, and there he was. Terribly and entirely and only Constantine, filling the whole frame. He was in pajamas. The sight of him in a threadbare T-shirt and sweatpants made me feel such a tenderness in the pit of my stomach and the palms of my hands that I forgave him for almost everything, at once.

"Ocean," he said, surprised.

I was horrified. I should have responded in the document. I should have told him I was coming, or at least when I would be back. What had possessed me to show up on his doorstep unannounced?

But then he grinned. "Ocean, hi. I thought you were the food delivery guy, but you're much better. You just got back?" He stepped aside to let me into the building. He lived six floors up but there was no elevator, he said. He had pulled three all-nighters in just the last week to meet a deadline on his thesis, which he was doing on the philosopher Emil Cioran, and so now he was sleeping in fourteen- or fifteen-hour bouts, which he woke up from to order food and watch episodes of shows he'd neglected for weeks. He couldn't stop yawning; he yawned every six or seven words.

"This is me," said Constant, when at last we reached the right landing. He corralled me through the door into an extraordinarily messy apartment. I didn't know where to look. There were clearly too many objects vying for square footage, and none of it was furniture; instead, precarious stacks of books lined all four walls, on top of which sat grocery bags and old *New Yorker*s and a record player in a suitcase. A TV sat on a collapsible chair ringed by other mismatched collapsible chairs. Constant led me down a narrow path through the living room, weaving around a number of large trash bags filled with clothing.

"Sorry about this," said Constant. "None of my roommates are back yet, but one of them is moving out as soon as he gets here. He's packing." He gestured at the trash bags. "Or he's embraced a minimalist lifestyle, I don't really know. How was your Christmas?"

He opened the last door. Inside, it was so dark it took my eyes a minute to adjust. Constant had blackout curtains drawn over the single window; it was dark as midnight, though the sun hadn't yet set. Here it was less messy but no less crowded. There were several more leaning towers of books, a messy desk, a beanbag, and a recently vacated bed. Above it, on a shelf, were what looked like several Geiger counters and dozens of spray paint cans. At the foot of the bed, a projector sat on its rear and played a movie on the ceiling. Above the desk, there was a large flag embroidered with Greek letters.

I gestured at it. "Are you in a fraternity?"

Constant frowned. "Well," he said. "It's supposed to be a secret."

"That you're in a frat?"

"No, the society is secret." He said "society" like it was the opposite of fraternity.

He changed the subject. "I was sleeping," he said. "I was up for twenty-nine hours. I started hallucinating that I had turned into a beetle, in this box of a room—"

A bell rang, shrill, screaming, unnaturally loud in the dark. I jumped.

"Sorry," he said again. "That's the food. The buzzer's annoying, isn't it? I'll be right back."

Like that he left me alone in his room. My stomach dropped through my shoes. I didn't know where to look, so I sat at the edge of the bed and looked at my hands, and then I looked up at the ceiling. The projector had fallen asleep and a logo was bouncing around a blue rectangle high above my head. The room was small but the ceiling was almost absurdly high, so the space was taller than it was wide. Constant seemed to be gone for an unnaturally long time, but then he was back, hauling an enormous bag of food.

"No, sit," he said, when I jumped up. I didn't. I helped him shift things around on his desk until he had unloaded a small feast of Mediterranean food. He yawned again, so widely I could see a filling in his back tooth. Then he went to the bed and collapsed into it, which jolted the projector back to life. A movie started playing on the ceiling: a bar at the bottom said *The Lobster*. I didn't see how that could just be coincidence.

"Look," said Constant, pressing the heels of his hands into his eyes. "I'm really sorry." I had never seen him less eloquent. "Do you mind? I just need a few minutes. I can almost keep my eyes open. I'm really close." He was mumbling, almost incoherent. "Here, come sit, I'll play the movie for you. I just need a minute, honestly."

He fumbled around for his phone, and the movie started again. It took me a minute to muster up the courage to go perch on the side of his bed. By the time I did, he was already asleep. He was almost too big for the bed: he slept on a slight diagonal, and still his toes hung off the edge. His mouth was slightly open. His black curls had fallen all over his face. I couldn't look at him for another moment; my chest was caving in.

The movie seemed to be about how love was absurd or unbearable, and all of the artificial things you would do to maintain a connection. After a while my neck hurt from looking up. With as little movement as I could manage, I scooted back on my elbows. I felt Constant nudge a pillow under my head. I almost fell off the bed.

When I looked at him, he was smiling. His eyes were still

closed. "Come here," he said. His voice was thick with sleep. "The whole point of putting the TV on the ceiling is to be comfortable while you're watching, yeah?"

But I couldn't settle back into the pillow until he was sound asleep again. The movie ended and another played from the queue. This one turned out to be about someone lost in a dream, moving from one philosophical conversation to another, and full of false awakenings. I looked at Constant. Had he known I was coming? Was he trying to tell me something? He slept on. I could tell he was dreaming by the way his eyes moved behind his eyelids. He felt so far away that I didn't feel shy about looking at him anymore. A wave of sentimental exhaustion moved over me. Constant's room was warm and dark; the world felt very distant. Far away, on the ceiling, someone said something about bridges and Lorca, then, "Life is not a dream. Beware. And beware. And beware."

I didn't know I had fallen asleep until Constant was waking me. I opened my eyes. We had fallen asleep face-to-face, our noses almost touching. Constant's eyes were startling: they were qing. I wanted so badly to touch the hollows of his cheeks, so I did, fitting my palm to his jaw, my thumb on his cheekbone. He was so warm. Neither of us was fully awake. I felt only a little less than delirious when he put his hand over mine.

I knew, suddenly, what was going to happen next. I felt it like a premonition at the backs of my knees and in a line from my sternum to my pelvis. I still had my coat on; he was laughing at it, the enormous yellow puffer, unwrapping me or trying to, until we were both tangled in the sleeves. My head was spinning. The coat, at last, came off. I started shivering without it. Above us, the movie kept playing, scenes melting inexplicably into other scenes, filling the whole room with the attributes of dreaming. *Nothing is real,* I thought, and then, with despair, *Everything is real, all of this is happening.*

What no one had told me about sex was that it didn't occur all at once, but rather it was something that gathered momentum, like Sisyphus's boulder once he lost his grip. If I did want to slow down, I wanted it with less urgency than it would take to stop a moving train in its tracks. I had crossed some threshold of no return long before we were undressing. Then he was kissing my collarbones. I could feel my heart beating against his lips. He had taken his shirt off; his bare chest was so beautiful, the squarish lines of his pectorals, the way his shoulders met his arms. There was a freckle at the base of his throat, with a single fine hair. All my limbs felt waterlogged.

"I've never done this before," I managed to say, at some point.

"Okay," said Constant. "Okay."

I couldn't say what I was feeling. It hurt a little, but my endorphins and other natural opioids were swirling around and confusing the issue. I couldn't stop thinking about lobsters, and suffering. Lobsters, as far as we knew, had none of these natural opioids, which mostly belonged to mammals. They had nothing to mediate the sensation of pain. In the ocean, they were so sensitive to temperature that they could tell if the water changed by even one or two degrees, which meant that the worst thing we could possibly do to a lobster was boil it alive. I knew there was something wrong with me, that you weren't supposed to think about lobsters during sex. But I couldn't stop. I hoped I would not be reborn as a lobster, or as anything at all. The whole time Constant was above me, I felt more embarrassed than anything else, more embarrassed than I'd ever been in my life, and I had to close my eyes because I couldn't bear to look at him.

After, he kissed me for a long time. It felt really nice, but I still kept my eyes closed, and felt exhaustion soaking into my bones. If I could have wished for one thing, I would have teleported myself home to Brooklyn, and fallen asleep in my own bed.

Instead, Constant dug into the cold Mediterranean food and put on yet another movie. This one was in Czech, with English subtitles, and was about two girls, both named Marie, who decide to be sad in the first scene. From then on, they spent the whole movie either eating food or destroying it. Was Constant telling me something, about me, about sadness? Constant had a lot to say about the Czechoslovakian New Wave movement, and then about authoritarian regimes.

I nibbled on a kefta kebab and tried to stay awake.

"What's wrong?" he asked.

He said it really gently; it made me want to cry. After a moment, when I didn't answer, he put his arm around me. I rested my face on his shoulder, in the dip beneath his collarbone, where my cheek fit perfectly. He smelled warm and slightly spicy, like wood in the afternoon sun. When he held me, he wrapped his arm all the way around me and put his hand across my belly. It made everything else worth it.

"What are you thinking about?" Constant said, later.

I was thinking about how you had to trust what people were telling you; you had to trust that they were telling the truth. All along, he had been telling me to take him for his actions and not his words, because words could mean anything at all. Suddenly I felt so stupid I couldn't breathe. Part of avoiding pain was avoiding painful thoughts, Constant had said, but I couldn't seem to manage that. I was trying really hard not to cry, tilting my head back into Constant's shoulder as though the tears might fall back into my head. A stream leaked from the corner of my left eye. Constant didn't notice, not even when it soaked into his pillow. I was both relieved and hurt by this, that he hadn't noticed.

"What did you think of the movie?" Constant asked.

"Which one?"

"The first one," he said. *The Lobster.*

I thought about it. "I thought the director had a point," I said finally. "I think love is mostly about finding commonality, which isn't so hard to adopt, or fake. I think you would do just about anything for love."

"Me?" said Constant. I didn't need to look at him to know he was grinning. I could feel it in his body, and in my own. "Or you?"

I was instantly hurt. In his dark room, pressed against his bare chest, both loving him and being willing to do anything felt absurd.

"Constant?" I said. "Can I ask you something?"

I felt his chin tilt down, graze the top of my head. I was looking at the line of dark hair that extended down the middle of his chest to his belly. "Don't you usually call me Constantine?"

I swallowed. "Yeah," I said. "But I usually think of you as Constant."

Again, he was amused. "Why?"

Wasn't it obvious? "There's a disconnect between how I think and what I say."

We were both quiet for a beat. Constant said, "You can always ask me anything."

I took a deep breath. "Why did you write to me about your dream?" I said. "That first time, why did you write to me? What were you trying to tell me?"

He leaned his cheek against me, thinking. I felt the

cheekbone I so adored dig into the crown of my head. "Because you were in it," he finally said. "Somehow, it felt like everything was about you. You were all I could think about. The train wasn't essential, you see? Only you were. Only telling you was."

He said it so easily, without embarrassment at his own vulnerability. Then I realized he still hadn't exactly answered my question, or at least not in the way I'd meant it. As always, his answer was so smooth that I nearly missed the way he sidestepped the question. I wanted to know what expectations he had when he wrote—if he wanted me to write back, if he thought he would ever see me again. I wanted to know if he ever thought we would end up here when he wrote to me about his dream. My throat closed. Suddenly I felt exactly as I had on the edge of the water tower, or the edge of any roof, looking down. I felt like I couldn't bear this another minute. My eyelids were so heavy. I dreaded the cycle of things: waiting for Constant to write, being pulled again and again into his orbit, only to be flung around until I was physically nauseous, feeling elated by scraps. I was overwhelmed by just how much I wanted all of this to be over. I wished we had never met; then I wished to see him every day for the rest of my life.

"Do you want to spend the night?" Constant asked.

I wanted to go home. My head hurt again, not like a migraine, but like I had gotten off a roller coaster that kept bashing my skull into the seat. "I really need to take a shower."

He laughed. "I have a shower."

He reached over and brushed a strand of hair out of my face. *I could never say no to him,* I thought with despair. It got stuck in my throat every time. Instead I just stayed still, in his arms. The movie played on. Constant talked about the Velvet Revolution for a while, but then he got quiet, and I could tell he was falling asleep. His body became heavier on the mattress, and every once in a while he twitched violently. Eventually the movie ended and left us in the dark. I could still see his face, but only because I had already memorized it. I touched his hair, the smallest strand by his left ear. It was soft as down.

As slowly as I could, I crept out of his bed and got dressed. I felt better once I had put on my coat. I couldn't stay here. The idea of waking up beside him again mortified me. But after I put on my shoes and closed his door behind me, my whole body could recognize that something was ending. I stumbled down the six flights, and walked to the subway, and sat on a bench. I kept looking over my shoulder, hoping despite reason that he would come after me, and say all the right things. But wasn't that just the problem? There were no right things to say; there was nothing left. The train came. I cried the whole ride home.

THE PECULIAR AGONY OF CONTAINING MULTITUDES

For days I lay in my apartment and thought about Constant. Each day, when I didn't hear from him, it hurt a little more. Sometimes it felt unbearable to be alive, but sometimes I found a small, detached space where I could marvel at how affected I was, how much it hurt. I thought about how he had kissed my body, how he had held me in his arms, and I thought again and again, *It couldn't have meant nothing.* I couldn't have misinterpreted what had happened so egregiously.

Still, he didn't write anything in the document, or even open it. He didn't text or call, of course, since it was clear that we would never exchange numbers. My whole body ached from knowing this.

When the other pain came, it was so strange I didn't recognize it. I had never felt anything like it. I became physically aware of my bladder, even the shape of it at the base of my pelvis, and had to go to the bathroom several times an hour, though I could pass very little urine. It didn't exactly burn, and it was not exactly sharp or shooting, so I dismissed it and went back to bed. I kept falling asleep because being awake was so miserable. Neither Tashya nor Georgie were back yet from the holidays. The days lost all distinction. I kept the curtains drawn. Whenever I woke up, I checked the document to no avail, foraged for old frozen food, checked the document again, and went back to sleep.

At least now I knew why he was avoiding the document. I had looked up the college calendar and knew when the study-abroad students had to come back to campus for spring semester. It was the day after I had gone to Constant's apartment. I cried about this too, and then I tried to get used to the fact that I would probably never hear from him again, open relationship or not. Still, it was hard not to wonder if I had done something wrong while sleeping with him, or by sleeping with him. I wondered if he was hurt that I had snuck out, and then I felt cheered by the thought that maybe I had the power to hurt him, and then I was ashamed of myself. I recounted the day over and over in my head; I even watched one of the movies he had played on the ceiling. I broke down and read through our entire edit history, everything he had ever written to me. I forgot all of my dreams as soon as I woke up.

The pain—the second, stranger one—got worse. It felt like something was trying to cut me in half. I had to pee ten times an hour. I was too miserable to figure out what to do. *I shouldn't have had sex with Constant,* I thought again and again. I wasn't sure if I had liked it; I wasn't sure if that was even the issue. I couldn't think about it, his dark room and the way he touched me, and how after I had cried, at least not without feeling so humiliated that I wanted to jump off the roof just so I didn't have to deal with it anymore. But by that point my bladder hurt too much to get out of bed.

I heard someone opening the apartment door. I wondered if someone was breaking in, and then I decided I didn't care. But it was only Georgie. I could tell by the way she stomped around the kitchen singing along to whatever she was blaring through her headphones. It didn't sound like she was alone; she kept talking to someone who didn't respond, and her footsteps were followed by a strange jingling that I couldn't identify. Then she burst into my room, saw me, and screamed.

"Ocean," she gasped. "Oh my god. I didn't know you were back! Can I borrow your black jacket, the denim one? Ugh, it's really musty in here. Should I open a window?"

Behind her, silhouetted in the doorway, were the dogs. I blinked several times. I was sure I was dreaming.

"Oh," said Georgie. "Yeah, I stole the dogs. Honestly, I had to. Pushkin bullies Dostoyevsky when he's bored, and he's always bored—Dad and Harold are, like, never home. They have a walker who comes and takes them around the

block with seven other dogs, and there's this little bull ter-
rier that bullies Dos too. Anyway, Dostoyevsky is so fun
to walk—people freak out when they see him. You wanna
come walk him with me? Everyone is either giddy that he's
such a giant or they literally cross the street so they don't
get attacked." Georgie snorted. "Even though Pushkin is
obviously the vicious one. You know, I really think that if I
died in front of Pushkin, he'd start eating me before I even
got cold." She glared down at Pushkin, who was sniffing at
the threshold of my door. Dostoyevsky sat politely behind
Georgie, his tail mopping the kitchen floor. "Anyway, the
jacket? I think I might go to Bushwick tonight, you want
to come?"

She flicked on the light switch. I moaned. The light made
everything worse. It was easier to bear it all in the dark.

"Ocean, oh my god," said Georgie. "Jesus Christ, are you
okay? What's wrong? How long have you been here?"

All language had left me. There was only sensation; all
sensation was dreadful. Experience was the problem that language could not communicate. I didn't want to be conscious
anymore. I shook my head.

"Ocean," said Georgie. Pushkin started barking. Even
Dostoyevsky looked concerned, his enormous face drooping,
his eyes as sad as those of God. "Tell me what's wrong."

"It's impossible," I managed.

"What is? What's impossible?"

"Life," I said. "It contradicts itself."

I couldn't go on. I couldn't tell her what was wrong, since there were no words for what I was feeling, and any approximation was useless. *Whereof one cannot speak,* I thought, again and again. Where I could not speak, there was only silence.

"Ocean," said Georgie, "if you don't tell me what's going on, I'm going to call Harold the neurosurgeon and put you in a car to the hospital."

"I don't need the hospital." Though I was being cleaved in two.

"Then tell me what's happening," said Georgie. She went to the kitchen for a cup of water and made me drink it, then sat at the edge of my bed. The dogs gathered around, making the room feel very small. What could I tell her? That I had lost any ability to speak? That there were no real words for pain?

"My pee hurts," I said.

"Oh," said Georgie after a beat, when it was clear I couldn't manage to say anything more useful. "Okay." Her brows were drawn low. "Okay. Does it feel like someone is taking a chainsaw to your vagina every time you pee?"

I blinked at her. It was exactly what it felt like.

"Okay," she said again. "Can you walk to urgent care with me? I think you probably have a urinary tract infection. Actually, I think I can do this online. God, am I glad that we live in a year where drugs come from the internet."

You could do anything over the internet, I thought. That was where everything important happened: in the cloud.

For several minutes, Georgie fumbled around on her phone while I lay as still as I could, trying to contain the pain. She went through my backpack and found my ID, yelling at Pushkin the whole time, who was trying to rip open an old granola bar he'd found under my bed.

She kept asking about my symptoms. Was the pain itchy or burning? Did the pain come in waves or in bursts? I didn't know what any of the words meant. I felt really gloomy about this, since I wanted medication, not sedatives. In the end, Georgie handled the whole thing, and a virtual doctor sent a prescription to the nearest pharmacy. "Honestly," she said, "Harold the neurosurgeon could have just written me a prescription, but it was probably better not to get him involved."

I could feel Georgie's questions looming; I knew as soon as we solved this, she would want to know why my urinary tract was infected, and who had infected it. I also didn't want to get Harold the neurosurgeon involved.

"I'll go get the meds," she said. When I tried to protest, she waved me off. "I have to walk Pushkin again anyway. I'll leave you with Dostoyevsky, though, he'll be nice."

And Dostoyevsky was. After Georgie left, he climbed onto the other side of my bed and was so enormous he took up most of it. He let me stroke his fur, which was so silky that the sensation of it almost balanced out the pain.

"Dostoyevsky," I whispered. "Am I dead?"

He sniffed my hair. He let out a low, ambiguous whine, and then settled beside me. Eventually we both fell asleep in the dark.

Georgie came back with antibiotics and painkillers. The painkillers turned my urine bright orange, like soda. I moved to Georgie's room, which was cleaner than mine and didn't smell so bedridden. Dostoyevsky stayed behind, since neither of us could convince him to move, and slept on. In Georgie's south-facing bedroom, the sun painted the walls gold. I took her papasan chair, which sat in the bay window and was warm from the light. She curled up on her bed with Pushkin in her lap and looked at me. I braced myself.

"So," she said. "I broke up with Tash."

I blinked. "What?"

She blew out a whole lungful of breath, and then fell back across her bed, fully deflated. Before she turned her face away from me, she looked like she was about to cry. "I don't know," she said. "We weren't really talking. It was killing me. But the real problem is that Tashya doesn't think it's a problem. Our affection levels are, like, incompatible."

It was obvious that Georgie had convinced herself these things were true, though it seemed to me this wasn't an issue when they were in the apartment together, alternating bedrooms. There was less miscommunication when they were face-to-face. That was the problem with me and Constant. We managed to miscommunicate no matter what.

"So who put *you* in this state?" asked Georgie. "Was it the philosopher? Tashya told me. Don't be mad, I literally sat on her until she gave in. Or be mad, I guess I don't care anymore."

I chewed on my lip. I didn't want to tell Georgie what had happened; saying it out loud would make everything a thousand times worse. I could see now how extraordinarily stupid I had been at every possible turn: following Constant into the subway tunnels and writing essays to him, pining over him even after I found out he had a girlfriend, having sex with him when really all I wanted was for him to tell me that he liked me back.

Georgie took a look at my face and shook her head. "Ocean, listen to me," she said severely. "You can't sleep with philosophy majors. I'm serious. Or econ majors, or poets. You have to find yourself a nice geology major. Those are usually fine. Literature majors are assholes, even if they love Mary Oliver. And *never* hook up with a history major." Georgie shuddered. "Anyway, men in general are the bottom half when it comes to being good in bed. Now, girls in philosophy—that's a different story."

I was morose. "But he was my first time," I said. "I don't really have any context."

Georgie was intrigued. "Really? That was your first time

having sex? Sorry," she said quickly, seeing my expression. "I don't actually mean anything by that, I just didn't know. So when are you going to see him again?"

"Never." As soon as I said it, I knew it was true. His girlfriend was back; he was probably with her now. He hadn't kept writing in the document, like he said he would, which also meant that he had lied when he told me he'd miss me. It hadn't taken long at all for him to forget me.

"He hasn't texted you?" Georgie propped herself up on her elbows to look at me. "Have you texted him?"

"No," I said. It was all about to come out. "He's actually never texted me."

"What do you mean?"

"I don't have his phone number."

"What? This was a one-night stand?"

"No," I said, and then I started to cry. "I've known him for months. We met that night the power went out." Georgie peered at me, not saying anything, so I had to continue. "He found me in the subway and made me look at the sky. We graffitied a tunnel."

Even as I said it, I could hear how disjointed it was, how little sense I was making. Georgie was frowning, and she was only going to keep frowning. "How the hell do you guys get in touch with each other? The post office?"

"Not the post office," I said miserably. "The cloud. We write to each other in this document."

"What?" said Georgie. There wasn't any judgment in her voice; she just sounded baffled. "Why?"

"I don't know," I said. "It's just how we started talking, in these letters, and it just kept going."

"But why? What do you even write to each other about?"

I shrugged and wiped my eyes. "There's more room to think, I guess. Like in the document, instead of over text. You can really write out everything you're thinking. And I guess—*everything*. We talk about everything. Philosophy of self and free will and the meanings of words."

Georgie was increasingly suspicious. "What do you mean, the meanings of words?" she said. Her voice was getting higher, the same way my mother's did. I started to feel tense again. "Which words?"

"I don't know," I said. "All of them. The way all words contain each other. If you open up a dictionary to look up one word, you might have to look up another word in its definition, and then another word in *that* definition, and you could just go on and on forever. And then it seems like words don't have any real meaning at all, and communication is a really futile project. What?" I said, defensive, seeing her expression.

"Ocean," she said, "is that why you couldn't tell me what was wrong with you? Oh god, is that why you were so quiet before Christmas?"

"I wasn't quiet."

"You could hardly string a sentence together! That was

because of this guy, this philosopher? He made you forget how to talk?"

"I wish you'd stop calling him that," I said, distressed that she was distressed. "His name is Constantine." Saying his name out loud was physically painful.

"Constantine," scoffed Georgie. "That's already a red flag." I didn't say anything. But Georgie was relentless. "So let me guess. He tells you some bullshit about existence, the whole breakdown of the universe, and he convinces you that there's something more *real* than our senses have access to, until you stop seeing trees and houses and people and start seeing atoms, and thinking none of this is real, all of this is illusion. Your eyes stop adjusting, and everything goes out of focus until he's the only thing in the frame. That's it, right? That's what it was like? God, Ocean. You don't trust yourself enough to call someone else on their bullshit. *That's* your problem. I love calling people out on their bullshit, and Tashya is so above bullshit from the start, but you—you always entertain the possibility that *you* might be wrong, even about really basic things like pain, or love. Ocean. You absolute nut."

She looked at me with such affection and understanding that I wanted to crawl out of my own skin. It was worse than pity—it was worse even than if she didn't care. Georgie looked like she knew exactly how I felt. Now we were both feeling this monstrous thing: it had doubled. "It wasn't like that," I wanted to say, except of course it was almost exactly like that. Georgie identified it in me as easily as Constant had—that I didn't understand what people meant when they called themselves grounded or authentic or alive, like at any moment I was prone to fade right out of existence. I looked wretchedly at my hands, waiting for them to go transparent. I had never felt more like a ghost, and at the same time more trapped in my own body.

"It doesn't even matter," I said eventually. *I'm the flight risk, I think.* It was one of the first things he'd ever said to me. I hated myself. I should have known this was going to happen. I should have been prepared. "We're done talking. He has a girlfriend."

Georgie softened. She sighed and climbed out of her bed. She crossed the room and squished herself into the other half of the papasan chair and put an arm around me. I started crying again; it felt so good just to be held by another person.

"Jesus, Ocean," she said, but it was sympathetic, not exasperated. "He really makes you want to kill yourself, huh?"

I could tell she meant it lightly, but I said, "Yeah," and meant it.

Then Georgie didn't say anything for a long time. I knew I should reassure her. There was still time to laugh it off. But I couldn't—when Constant didn't respond, or whenever he left me, I had wanted to kill myself. Whenever he put me on a train, or left me on one, it felt like he took all the oxygen in the world with him, in his pockets. And then what was the point? At first, when I met him, he'd made me feel really alive, until he was the only thing that made me feel alive. Or maybe that wasn't even true—maybe it was just that when I was around him, I didn't care. I didn't care about anything, I just wanted him to look at me, and grin. Was this love? The serious pain, the weight on the brain?

"Sometimes," Georgie said at last, in a small voice, "when I feel myself getting heavy, like really depressed, I can go to this space where it hurts a little less." The room had gone really quiet. The light had changed; the sun was leaving. "As far as disassociating goes, it seems at least a little productive to take a step back, and look at the place where it hurts, and why, and who hurt you." She glanced at me. "You know what I mean?"

For a moment, I was tempted to come clean, and show Georgie all the things Constant had written to me. I thought about the way we, Constant and I, had talked about pain: how I thought of pain as something I didn't know how to talk about, and how Constant thought it wasn't worth words. By then the UTI had stopped hurting so urgently, so I could see what Georgie meant. Only after it had ended could I recognize how much it had hurt, and why the unfamiliar pain had taken me so long to identify, and how this pain and other ones seemed to originate around Constant.

Before I could say anything else, Dostoyevsky nosed his way into the room and stopped just inside, sniffing. He let out a great sigh before padding across the hardwood to fall asleep again in the last patch of sun. Georgie and I stayed curled on top of each other, ruminating on our own heartbreaks, until the room went blue, then dark. Time passed. I woke up in the middle of the night with an excruciating crick in my neck, but less pressure on my chest.

A few days later, Tashya came back. I didn't see her before she left again for the conservatory. After, I could hear Georgie slamming the fridge door and muttering in the kitchen. I pretended to be asleep when she barged into my room. I felt sorry after she left, because then she was so quiet I knew she had to be really devastated. I stared at my ceiling and dreaded this new state of our lives, where my roommates both yearned for and despised each other.

I shouldn't have worried. Late that same night Tashya crept in and went straight to Georgie's room, where I heard them murmuring all night. Even when they communicated only in ultimatums, they still understood each other better than Constant and I did with our thousands and thousands of words. In the morning, they both came to wake me so we could go get bagels.

It snowed every day for a week and a half straight. All sorts of words were floated around, none of which seemed to have much meaning: nor'easter, snow squall, blizzard-force winds. I took my antibiotics and tried to check the untitled document no more than three times a day, though I almost always exhausted this before breakfast. Georgie kept trying to engage me in activities, like walking the dogs despite the weather, or venturing to the gourmet grocery to marvel at the size of the sumo oranges, or painting our faces with vibrant makeup and taking pictures in her room. Tashya was still trekking to the conservatory through several feet of snow, until one night she came home frosted white head to toe, gasping.

"Thomas Sato lives right by campus," she said angrily, wiping snowflakes from her eyelashes and trailing mascara down her face. "Like, a block away. The whole building's empty, he's going to stay there all night, and no one else can even practice. I don't think I can go again until the snow stops. I couldn't even see when I was walking back from the station. The train got stuck crossing the bridge and two separate girls in my car had panic attacks."

So Tashya stayed home with us too, which Georgie was so unaccustomed to that she became positively giddy. At night, Georgie made us turn off all the lights and roast s'mores on the stove, and a wayward marshmallow almost set the whole apartment on fire. Tashya tapped her fingers against any flat surface; sometimes I woke up in the middle of the night to hear the rhythm of her concerto against the kitchen laminate.

Then we literally ran out of food. We had been subsisting

on frozen dumplings, frozen tamales, and a rotating schedule of takeout. One afternoon it snowed a whole foot in four hours, so getting delivery was out of the question, and when Georgie went to paw through the fridge, she screamed so loudly Tashya hit herself in the face with the door in her haste to run to her, and the dogs yapped their heads off and Dostoyevsky upended the table on which we stacked the pots.

"What?" asked Tashya, clutching her nose. "What happened?"

"We're out of food!" cried Georgie. "We're literally out of food!"

It was not strictly true. There was a bag of frozen peas, half a box of vegetable stock, and a lemon. In the cabinets, we found a box of instant rice. Georgie was still hysterical. "We're going to starve!" she wailed. "Society is falling apart at the seams!"

It took Tashya a while to calm her down. In the end what comforted her was the reminder that, at least, she still had weed. She went to her room to self-medicate. In the kitchen, Tashya did something miraculous with the peas and boxed rice until Dostoyevsky and Pushkin were sniffing hopefully at the air. She retrieved Georgie and sat us all down at the table, and presented an ugly risotto that tasted much better than it looked.

"It's vegan," said Georgie sadly.

• • •

The next day the snow stopped. Soon there were occasional, astonishing breezes that smelled like spring.

Day after day I could only think about the water tower, and about Constant. Whatever ambition had convinced me to defer my schooling in order to work on myself had vanished. All I wanted was Constant, and this made me wish I were dead. I couldn't believe he was really gone because I knew *exactly* where he was, staring at his projector-lit ceiling at an address he'd given me. But he was gone from me, because he was gone from the document. The document began to feel sinister, as though our relationship was akin to the one between the scientist and the wasp. Even that wasn't quite right. I wasn't even the wasp—I was the cricket, a prop in the experiment, with the least agency of all. I thought a lot about gravity; I thought how you could know all there was to know about gravity, all the complicated math and physics, and still it was theoretical until you were falling. It was like the black-and-white room that Constant had written of. There was something to be said for experience. In the long hours when Georgie and Tashya were occupied with each other and at last left me alone, it was all I could think about: the fine line between life and death. I lay awake long into the night and thought about this with my eyes closed in the dark, until I lost all sense of my body, and I was floating in space.

Constant never appeared on the document again. His last time stamp was dated the night I had visited his apartment. His last paragraph, on the meaninglessness of pain, remained above a great expanse of white screen like stagnant water. Every time I saw it, I felt sick to my stomach, but I couldn't help but look at it several dozen times a day to reassure myself that Constant was real, that what we had done was real and the places we had visited were real too. In the worst hours, I thought, how could he disappear so suddenly and so entirely, when he *knew* it would make me wonder if it had all been a delusion? If it had all been real, how could he just leave? I could remember every time he touched me, from the first hand he extended to me in the subway station, how our faces had been so close together in the dark. I thought of how he had held me, that day in his apartment, the way his arm wound around my entire middle and his whole hand covered my belly, the way he had kept adjusting me closer. If all those things had really happened, how could he just disappear?

It seemed like I might live like this forever, in this hideous cycle. Georgie and Tashya kept saying both obliquely and directly that eventually enough time would pass, and it would begin to hurt less. Georgie, finally, said I had to get over myself and sleep with someone else. Tashya said all pain gets absorbed into your body—it never goes away, but in time you stop feeling it. But they were both wrong. The pain was like a leech, foreign and not quite part of me. It too belonged to the document. I was going to love Constant forever; I was doomed.

I thought about deleting the document. I thought about changing the name of the document so Constant would get a notification; I could title it SHOUTING INTO THE VOID or EXPIRED DOCUMENT or even ARE YOU GHOSTING ME? I thought about the sometimes girlfriend, and realized that she was actually *always* his girlfriend—*I* was sometimes. Sometimes I was Constant's friend and sometimes he had no words to describe me, but I was only occasionally a phenomenon in his life, and he in mine.

THE GUTTER

Tashya's concert, it turned out, was not a concert but a competition, in a small upstairs space at Carnegie Hall. The winner would get to perform with the New York Philharmonic in the summer, at an outdoor concert in Central Park. We took a train into Manhattan. Tashya sat sandwiched between Georgie and me. Tashya was so tense she didn't say a single word for most of the ride but kept her eyes closed and her fingers tapping forcefully against her thighs. I could tell she was infecting Georgie with nerves because when we were a few stations away, Georgie blurted out, "Good thing you don't have stage fright like me. But should we go find somewhere for a few shots before this thing just in case?" Then they bickered (Tashya said) because Georgie called Tashya's competition a *thing*, and (Georgie said) because Tashya was neurotic. We got off at the wrong station, and Tashya walked several feet in front of both of us for the extra ten blocks, and barely allowed us to wish her good luck before she left us at the door.

Georgie and I debated whether to sit in the front row. Would it be better for Tashya to see familiar faces, or would that be even more nerve-racking? In the end we settled on the third row, half illuminated by the stage lights. We found Tashya's name in the program, smack in the middle of twenty or so others, and then we penciled malignant wishes around Thomas Sato's.

The competition was extraordinarily long. All the music was phenomenal, but each performance lasted at least ten minutes. Georgie kept trying to check her phone on the sly, and three different ushers came to chastise her. During the intermission, the line for the bathroom was so long we ended up running to the diner across the street.

Tashya was the first to play after intermission. She appeared in a red dress that made Georgie gasp so loudly several people shushed her. "You shut up," Georgie hissed back. "That's my *girlfriend*." I could see Tashya trying not to smile; they had forgiven each other. She took a seat and adjusted the piano bench. For several long moments, she settled herself. And then she began to play.

I had never heard Tashya actually play before. I had heard her practice; I had heard some measures a hundred or so times. But I had never seen her perform. Tashya, unlike Georgie, was really good at performing. She gave the impression of having been swallowed by the music:

nothing could touch her. I could see now what she meant that day she was so upset about touching keys. Each note had to be precisely indented, in such a way that the long mallet within the body of the piano could strike the string with just the right intensity. I couldn't believe Tashya could memorize it. *All motion is impossible,* I marveled as I watched her hands move. I felt sort of in love with her, and with Georgie too, who was watching Tashya with her face uplifted and her expression sublime. There was no one like the two of them, I thought. I felt really happy to be there, just listening. We gave her a standing ovation, though at the beginning of the concert the conservatory director had begged everyone to hold their applause until the end, since there were so many performers.

Other musicians took the stage. After each of them Georgie leaned over to say, without any attempt to lower her voice, some variation of, "God, they just are not on Tash's *level.*" At last it was Thomas Sato's turn. He was really short, but in fact he played so well that even Georgie couldn't muster up anything snarky to say. She clutched my hand until the last musician had played their last note, and then we rushed back out to the lobby to find Tashya.

The results wouldn't be announced until the next day. Georgie fumed about this, but Tashya just seemed happy and relieved that it was over. She had achieved something, and she was satisfied. I couldn't stop looking at her. I tried to remember if I had ever had that feeling, which I could see so plainly on her face. I was so preoccupied I almost didn't see Constantine.

But then I looked up and he was there, on the other side of the crosswalk. He was wearing his peacoat and a scarf I had never seen. My lungs turned to liquid. I was going to vomit, or cry. I knew he'd seen me too, because I saw him freeze mid-sentence—he was with someone, but my vision had tunneled, and he was the only person on the planet. *Constant, Constant.* My whole body was singing it, every last cell.

The light changed. I couldn't move. But Constant was stepping off the curb, taking enormous steps. My life flashed before my eyes. It occurred to me that I was dreaming. It occurred to me that I had lost my mind. He was getting closer. My heart was in my throat and throbbing against my windpipe. I looked down the street. I could still run; I could just sprint, leaving Tashya and Georgie behind. But then Georgie noticed the walk sign and began towing Tashya and me into the crosswalk.

"Ocean," he said. *Ocean,* he said. It could mean a thousand or more things. It could mean nothing at all. *I should have run before the light changed,* I thought. *I should have thrown myself into traffic.*

"Hey," he said, and then he grinned. His hair was longer. The curls were falling into his eyes. His scarf was so vivid.

The pain I felt was unfamiliar and exquisite. "How have you been?" he said.

All understanding was impossible, and this was the nature of the world. Otherwise, how could he say that? How could he ask me, "How have you been?" Didn't he know I had been terrible? I knew they were all staring at me—Georgie and Tashya and Constant and the girl who was with him, his girlfriend. But I couldn't think of anything to say. I couldn't stop looking at his girlfriend, even though she was the last person I wanted to see. I couldn't believe it. She too was Asian. She was wearing a beautiful coat, and a hat in an improbable color. It was so clear that she wasn't afraid to be perceived—why should she be? Her hair was so healthy, and her manicure was fresh. How could she possess so many things I wanted, these things that were so impossible for me?

"You're in the gutter," Constantine said.

And like that I relented, and the lump in my throat burst from all the tenderness I felt. He was sympathetic; he understood. I nodded.

He laughed at me. "No," he said, and pointed at my feet.

I was standing in the street, in a dirty puddle of melted snow. I had worn nice, non-waterproof boots for the concert. The entire universe was conspiring to call me a fool.

"Ocean, *come on*," Georgie said, her tugging turning to hauling, and I almost tripped as she dragged me away. The abrupt and growing distance between Constant and me seemed like divine intervention: Georgie, my deus ex machina. My relief was short-lived—I turned my head and got an impression of oncoming headlights and a swerving biker screaming obscenities at my face. And then we were on the opposite side of the street. Georgie and Tashya were both panting beside me. I looked back across the canyon of speeding cars and felt a rush of joy to see him, still watching me.

I turned away and squeezed my eyes shut, so I didn't cry, so I didn't have to see him walking away with the girlfriend. It was so much worse than I'd ever imagined. My nose started to run. Georgie or Tashya or both were saying my name. I couldn't open my eyes. It was too hard to feel all the things I was feeling: humiliation and longing and loss and desire for him in his stupid scarf. Eventually Tashya and Georgie linked their arms through mine and led me to a different street. I had ruined the whole day.

On the train I kept thinking that there was something unrealistic about the way we had run into each other. Could I be uncannily prone to wretched luck? In low tones beside me, Tashya and Georgie concluded that we had run into *the* philosopher while I tried to tune them out.

"Well, he was really tall," Georgie said sympathetically, as if what had happened to me might have happened to anyone, because Constant was so tall. She rubbed my back. I felt the same way I always felt when I rode the train away from Constantine—too devastated to breathe. It was over.

• • •

And then he wrote back.

He didn't just write back, he changed the name of the untitled document to I MUST ASK YOU HOW YOU EXPERIENCE TIME, so I got an email about his edits. I was really annoyed that I hadn't beaten him to it. I refused to open the document for as long as I could. It was like holding my breath; I only lasted a few minutes. Then I skimmed his paragraph. He didn't acknowledge how long he had been silent, how he had shown all the signs of disappearing, how he had slept with me and fallen off the face of the earth. He didn't even mention how we had run into each other on the street two hours before. Instead, he wrote about fictive motion.

If I told you to meet me at midnight, and then changed my mind and asked to move our meeting forward by two hours, would you think we were meeting at ten, or at two? They say there are two ways that people think metaphorically about time. In the ego-moving metaphor, you think we're meeting at two: you are progressing toward the future. In the time-moving metaphor, you think we're meeting at ten: time is a conveyor belt on which you are stationary. This might be important to you, since it seems to be one of those instances wherein language affects (infects?) thought, and the way we talk about time changes the way you experience it.

The real problem of time, though, isn't a linguistic one. The faster you move through space, the slower you experience time. This is why a clock at the top of a mountain will move a fraction of a millisecond slower than a clock at sea level. At the top of a mountain, at the peak of the earth's curve, you are moving through space at a very slightly faster rate than you would be on the surface. Time and space curve where there is matter: everything bends toward the star. Einstein's girlfriend sits him down one night and says, "Albert, I need two things from you." Einstein says, "Yes, all right, what can I do for you?" The girlfriend says, "I just need some time and space." Einstein is politely puzzled, and hesitates a beat before he says, "Yes, and what is the second thing?"

When we say *time is passing*, it is a metaphor. Time does not pass; we are just falling. Time is our constitution. Time is the ocean within which we are all fish (or lobsters). Sometimes it feels like I saw you only a minute ago; sometimes it feels like an eon. Do you experience this too? You and I, we're hurtling through space, and around us time both puddles and clings. Physics is not interested in language; a lot of it falls to that of which we cannot speak. Writing to you is not the same as writing an equation. There is mistranslation and an inadequate connection between my mind and my hand, my mind and itself, my mind and your mind. You're right that sometimes we miss each other in our elliptical travels, and yet it still feels like we are orbiting the same thing, gradually falling closer.

All this to say: Ocean, Ocean, will you meet me two hours forward from midnight at Green-Wood?

I was so agitated I threw my phone down on the bed. It bounced off a pillow and landed on the floor. I paced my tiny room. I couldn't believe he had written. I couldn't believe he'd said nothing about anything that had happened, how we had run into each other on the street, how I had been unable to speak to him. It was as though it had never happened, or as though it meant something completely different to him than it had to me.

Of course I wouldn't go meet him. I wasn't even sure how I could, since there was no way to know what time he meant. Ten o'clock? Two o'clock? Obviously I saw myself as stagnant upon the conveyor belt of time, but it seemed likely that Constant was of the ego-moving metaphor—so what time did he mean? Was he accounting for my perception, or was I supposed to account for his? I wasn't even sure it was good physics. Why did he tell me the joke about Einstein's girlfriend? Who needed time and space—me? Him?

I read what he had written several more times. My heart soared every time I read my name. *Ocean, Ocean . . .* When I imagined him typing it out, his hands moving over the letters, it felt like he was touching me. But I could see what he was doing. I could recognize the way he maneuvered his words so he didn't have to apologize for disappearing but instead pondered over the perception of time. Individual lines overwhelmed me with a feeling that was sublime. *You and me.* I hated how happy those three words made me: just to group us as a unit, in letters, just to have that small proof that there really was a connection between us. The two of us in a dark subway station. I missed him fiercely.

I thought about how his back had looked while he was painting, how I could see the shape of his shoulder blades even through his windbreaker, and how much I had liked him even that first night. I kept thinking about how if I could go back in time, I would still follow him into the subway tunnel, which meant I had learned nothing at all. I had kept talking to him even after I learned he had a girlfriend, and I still wrote back to him every time he disappeared, and I still believed whatever he told me even though he thought of truth as essentially incompatible with language.

My phone rang. I dove for it, in case it was Constant, though he didn't even have my number. My phone had absolutely shattered when it hit the floor, and the screen was now spiderwebbed in cracks. It took me a second to even read who was calling: it was my mom. I was crushed. I ignored the call; I couldn't imagine lying to her right now.

But she called again, and again. My stomach began to twist. Something was wrong. She called another seven times in a row before she left a voice mail. My hands were shaking when I picked up my phone again to listen to it.

"Ocean," said my mother, tinny and tight in the recording. "Will you call me back? I just got an email from your school. I need to talk to you."

My mother had never been one to whom the words "I love you" came easily; in fact, before I was in middle school, she never said it at all. "I love you" isn't a phrase in Chinese the way it is in English. In Chinese, love, like pain and physics, was something too large for words. Casual language was insufficient; instead, we said nothing at all to each other on the subject of love. But by some time in middle school, I had picked up on this parental anomaly; I'd noticed I lacked the constant reassurance in a lunch-box note or at school drop-off, and brought it up to her. Since then, she had made a genuine but painful effort to say "I love you" to me, particularly over the phone, when we didn't have to make eye contact. At the end of the voicemail, it hadn't come. She'd said, "I need to talk to you," and hung up.

There. Everything was over. My mother knew—she knew I wasn't at school, that I had been lying this whole time. She was going to make me move home. I'd have to leave my sweet tiny apartment and Georgie and Tashya. I would never see Constant again. If I wasn't already dead, my mother was going to kill me. There was a sob in me that couldn't find enough oxygen to rise out of my mouth. What was I going to say to Benny, who I was supposed to see tomorrow? What would I do about my lease?

The sun was starting to set. Georgie and Tashya were both napping. They had told me to wake them up when I was ready to order food; we had decided to get pizzas from an overpriced wood-fired place, to congratulate Tashya on her performance and to console me. I felt like I would die if I kept sitting in my room, just watching as my life fell apart all around me.

My mother was calling again. I turned my phone off. Then I went to find Constant. I had to tell him I never wanted to hear from him again, even though I still loved him, and wanted no one else.

PURGATORY

Whether he meant ten o'clock or two o'clock, I was hours early. The day had been chilly, but the night was quickly growing frigid. The gates to the cemetery were open. I went in, because I knew the painter Basquiat was buried inside. I walked up a hill and found myself surrounded by headstones. Some were plain, but a great many were elaborate and enormous: obelisks like trees, weeping angels with folded wings, even pyramid mausoleums that seemed likely to end up in the next millennia's museums.

Night fell early and fast. Soon it was difficult to see where I was walking. I started back the way I'd come, but after several minutes, I still didn't see the entrance. I started to get worried that I had gotten turned around in the dark. It felt like the beginning of a horror movie.

At last the gothic spires of the gate came into view, faintly silhouetted against the bruise-colored sky. Behind it was Brooklyn, giving way to the harbor, a lone ferry, a weak moon. I shivered. My face was so cold it hurt. I had already decided to give him until ten. If Constant had meant for us to meet at two—well, then that was that and it was better for us never to see each other again. Even ten was pushing it.

But when at last I reached the gates, they were closed and locked. I tried not to panic. It was just past five, but there was no one in sight, and the guard vestibule was empty. By then it was totally dark, and the only lights were behind me, lighting a path through the cemetery. I kept turning my head; it was eerie, like the only way forward was backward, deeper into this dead place. I walked along the perimeter for a while, waving at security cameras, sure that someone would come yell at me but at least they'd let me out.

No one came. I didn't know what to do. Eventually I ended up back at the gate. Surely a security guard would arrive any minute. I crouched down and pulled my giant mustard coat over my legs and shoved my hands in my pockets. Maybe I wasn't meant to jump off anything after all; maybe I was meant to freeze here, like the matchstick girl, or become the first victim of zombies. I wasn't exactly afraid, but it was unsettling to be fenced in with several thousand dead people; it was like my circumstance was conspiring to cast doubt on my existence. What if I was here in the cemetery because I belonged in the cemetery? What if everything was a sign; what if none of this had ever been coincidence?

I was afraid to turn on my phone to see all the notifications from my mother. But I was getting really cold, and the wind was picking up. I needed help. I tried to click it on several times. Nothing happened. The screen remained dark and shattered. My phone had died in my pocket.

I started to panic. My chest ached; I couldn't breathe. I had to calm down; I was getting hysterical. But I couldn't stop thinking, *I don't know what to do, I don't know what to do,* in a terrible loop, so there was no room in my head to figure out my options. I couldn't look at my circumstances objectively, because I started hyperventilating every time I tried. I started crying because I was so fucking cold. My tears fell into my hair and froze.

How did I get myself into these messes? It seemed like no one else fainted up on top of water towers or got locked in cemeteries. Was this what Constant meant when he said strange things happened around me? That everything just went wrong for me? I always lost my head. I was useless under pressure. I was indecisive as a personality trait.

I didn't know how long I sat there. At some point I lost feeling in my thighs. Every time I tried to calm down and figure out what to do, I thought of my mother and felt the symptoms of a migraine. The fence was too tall to climb, but every few minutes I checked to make sure. I jumped in front of the security cameras again. They didn't even seem to be on. I needed to get somewhere warm. The street in front of the cemetery was deserted. Occasionally there was a car, but none of them slowed or saw me. I was stuck.

Until, of course, Constant appeared.

A flicker of light shone across the street. The cherry tip of a very small fire, hanging loosely from someone's mouth. I knew it was him. I knew by the way the tip of the joint moved; I recognized his gait.

"Constantine!" I screamed. "Constantine!"

He stopped dead in his tracks. The joint fell to the ground in a rush of sparks. He was just shy of the gate's lights. I couldn't quite see his face, but he was close enough now that I could make out the familiar beanstalk shape of him.

"What the hell," he murmured, and then, louder, "Ocean?"

He was wearing the scarf. He was holding a huge book, and I must have been close to delirious, because I thought he could break me out with it. For a moment he didn't move, just stood there, staring at me. He came right up to the gate and squinted down at me.

"Ocean," he said. He sounded amazed.

"Constantine," I said. My voice was choked and damp.

"You said you weren't from Green-Wood," he said. He sounded delighted.

I hiccupped. "I got locked in."

"How long have you been in there?" he asked. "A couple minutes? Centuries?"

"I'm not dead," I said, so annoyed I meant it. "Can you help me get out?"

He was squinting at the security cameras. "Hasn't anyone come to unlock the gate?"

I stared at him. "Obviously not." Then I felt bad for snapping at him, though he deserved it. "What's that?" I asked, pointing at his book.

"Just a reread," he said, considering me in his infuriating mild way. I wanted to snap at him again, but at the same time I reveled in the way he looked at me, the way he always did, a little bit astonished. There was this tenderness in his eyes, a sort of affection I felt all the way down my spine. I shivered.

"You're cold," he observed. "Here, hold this for a second?"

He handed the book through the bars. I took it. It was *Infinite Jest*. "You've just been, what, just lugging this around on the subway?"

"Sure," said Constant, undoing his scarf. "Here," he said.

I gave him his book back. The scarf was still warm when I wrapped it around my face. It smelled so much like him my eyes stung. I squeezed them shut. It seemed so ridiculous that all that was separating us was this gate, through which we could see each other and touch each other. I know that if I could just open it, my troubles would go away. Suddenly, all barriers seemed irrational and bureaucratic, something from an absurdist's dream.

"Kafkaesque," Constant observed.

I was startled. "You can read my mind?"

That made him laugh: his big, reverberant laugh. "If only. We could make this work, then."

He reached through the bars to tug on the scarf. I was going to cry again. I knew he could feel my breath in his palm. *We could make this work. His hands on my bare rib cage, my chest caving in.* He grinned. He *could* read my mind, I thought, and still this wasn't working.

"So," he said. "I think you'll have to climb over."

"I can't," I said. If I could, wouldn't I have done it already? "I'm not tall enough."

"I'll help you," he said. He looked again at the security cameras, two of which were pointed right at us. "I can't believe no one has come to let you out. Do you think the power's gone out again?"

I wouldn't have been surprised. I thought about what Constant had written about time, and how there were no adequate metaphors for it, but in my mind's eye I saw a spiraling barber's pole, infinite, and thought about how we always ended up where we began.

Constant knelt down close to the gate. Suddenly his face was much closer, at an angle I'd never seen him at before, where he was more vulnerable. I almost cupped his cheek before I could stop myself, just because I could reach it. I couldn't believe how much I liked his face.

"Okay," he said. "Stand on my leg. I'll keep you steady."

It seemed like such a large promise. But I put my boot on his knee. I remembered the pale inside of his thigh, and almost lost my balance. Constant put a steadying hand on my ankle.

It was no use. I still couldn't reach the top to pull myself over. I wasn't sure how Constant was envisioning this whole operation. I wondered what kind of upper body strength he imagined I had.

"Here, hop off," he said. I was already sliding. My cold feet hit the ground, and the jolt went all the way up my spine. He put *Infinite Jest* on his knee. "Okay, try this."

With the added three inches, I could reach the top. I still didn't know what to do next, since I wasn't capable of a single pull-up, and the spikes at the top of each bar made me nervous. Then Constant adjusted his leg and started lifting me higher. Through the bars, his hands came around my hips, and as he stood, I shot up on a slightly backward trajectory. Then I was clamoring over the top, headlong into Constant's arms. It was pure luck that we didn't both end up sprawled on the asphalt. Constant set me on my feet, and I immediately bent over coughing.

When I stood up straight again, I saw the way he was looking at me and was immediately aware that he was going to kiss me. His body leaned toward mine, like he couldn't help it. I stiffened; he saw. He caught himself. Time stuttered.

He fixed his scarf around my neck. "You should keep it," he said. "It looks good on you."

I was both crushed and relieved. I knew I couldn't go on like this, just pining. I had decided, when I left the apartment, that I was only coming to tell him that I couldn't see him anymore. Every time I saw or heard from him, I wanted to kill myself. I had to *stop* wanting to kill myself—that's why I was in the city, not at school.

He pulled the scarf up around my face. As he reached around to fix it so it covered the nape of my neck, he rested his hand on the back of my head, just briefly, in a way that felt as close to an apology as we would ever come. *Ocean,* he said, though he said it only with his body. *Ocean.* My whole skull fit in his palm. In the passing moment when he held me like that, it felt as though I had put my head down to rest; it felt like my heart was breaking.

Then Constant said, "Come on. Let's go paint a map."

We walked for what felt like a long time, though the train yard was just below the cemetery. Constant tried rubbing some warmth back into my shoulders, but it only made me shiver worse. We were both dragging our feet. The street was dark, and the streetlights seemed to grow weaker with each passing block. I was glad, because it meant Constant couldn't see my face. Probably we had only made it this long because we met each other almost exclusively in the dark. Finally Constant led me through a hole in a chain-link fence, into what looked like an unpaved parking lot. For the first time since summer ended, I was worried about rats. My eyes adjusted to the dark. There were three subway trains in front of us.

"I heard they keep some of the G trains here," said Constant. He led me to the nearest one, a hulking dark shape. "Hmm. These might be just here for storage. I think they pulled this model. Hey, did you know there used to be a V train?"

I shook my head.

"There used to be a 9 train, too," he said. "Here, set that over there." He handed me the Geiger counter and directed me to a low rock. Then he opened his coat, grabbed a can, and started painting.

I wondered when they had been dismantled. I wondered when, exactly, the V and the 9 ceased to be trains. On the side of the car before us, one by one, the remaining train lines appeared.

For ages we were quiet in the dark. Stars came out and disappeared again under the cloud cover. Far in the distance, a dog was barking.

Only when he got to the G line did Constant speak again. "That's why the G train is so short now," said Constant. "Because of the V train. You see that there are bigger problems than language. Just look at all these gaps the city decided not to fill."

I pictured workers in different MTA offices sending the wrong messages to the wrong people, while on some platform somewhere people accumulated until they were stacked to the dirty ceilings, waiting for trains that would never arrive.

"My girlfriend isn't very happy about this," said Constant in a conversational tone.

I felt my soul leave my body. *This is it,* I thought. This was my moment to say that I wasn't very happy about it either, and I didn't want to see him again. But "Why?" he would say, and I would crumble. Why? Because he treated me badly, and I let him. Because it wasn't sustainable; I couldn't bear it anymore. I wished I had never met him. But what was I supposed to do—how could I break up with someone I had never been dating in the first place? How could I tell him to stay away from me, when all I wanted in the whole world was for him to tell me he cared about me, and wanted to spend time with me, and liked me better than anyone else? *I don't want to see you anymore. I don't want you to write to me.* There it was—the language. All I had to do was say the words out loud, and then I could leave him in the dark lot, walk away, and get on a train and go home to eat pizza with Tashya and Georgie, and the nightmare would be over. I could go forth and live the rest of my life.

"She says it's bad for the environment," he said. "The aerosol."

It was difficult to put into words how much I hated her

then, the once and current girlfriend. For Constant, I felt something else. I leaned against the side of the train car and closed my eyes. The thing I felt was a lot like pain, at least in magnitude: it consumed me. It was shy of rage but stronger than longing. I felt it with my whole face. My bones felt pulverized from carrying the weight of my body for so many days in a row, feeling this feeling. I was so disappointed. I wanted so much for him to be a slightly different person, who liked me. I wanted it so badly it was astonishing and horrifying that I couldn't have it, and there was nothing to be done. I couldn't make Constant feel about me the way I felt about him. Life was full of things like this, things I wanted with an urgency that made my ears feel full of water and nonetheless I couldn't have. I wanted my mother not to have received whatever traitorous email she had received. I wanted to have more energy, and to sleep easier. I wanted to stop worrying about money.

What a stupid place, I thought. *And I can't even manage to get out of here.*

Constant had stopped painting. I couldn't quite see his face; there wasn't quite enough light. It didn't matter. I knew the exact shape of it. I could imagine his exact expression. His eyes were all over me. I could feel them like the light beam from his Geiger counter.

"Tell me what you're thinking about," he said. "I can never guess from your expression."

Why should I tell him? I couldn't remember when his opinion had come to mean so much to me.

"I was thinking about the way out of hell," I said eventually.

He laughed. It wasn't an unkind laugh; he laughed like he was delighted. "There *is* no way out of hell," he said. "Every system is outdated, and nearly all of them are unjust. Pleasure is fleeting. Money is plastic. The bees and the ice caps are gone. The worst has already happened. We're in hell anyway. So why not have some fun?"

I couldn't believe what he was saying, what he had been saying all along, which was that he didn't care that everything was shit. When he said *hell* he meant it purely philosophically—he wasn't actually suffering. For all he talked about nihilism, he wasn't prone to despair. I was the lobster in the pot, and he was the one writing the essay. All along, that was all we were. I tried to take a deep breath and couldn't, like there was a band around my chest. If I had been on any edge, I would have jumped. I would have done it, just to prove him wrong.

"Doesn't it ever occur to you that you're making it worse?" I asked. I tried to say it evenly; I really wanted to know the answer. "Doesn't that worry you? Like, what if you're having so much fun you knock over the rest of the dominos? What about monarch butterflies or, like, systemic racism? What about the other people in hell?"

"Hell *is* other people," he said. He was teasing because I was being magnanimous—but of course I wasn't talking about other people, I was talking about me. I had spent a lot of time agonizing about whether and when to write back, if I was annoying him, if it bothered him when I took too long to respond. Why wasn't he worried about making *my* life more painful and less bearable? How could you ask someone if they cared about you? How could you ask them to care, if they didn't already?

"Hey," he said. Whatever expression gripped my face made him soften his voice. "Hey, Ocean, I'm kidding."

But he wasn't kidding, not really. Constant thought this was hell because everything tended toward entropy—if you left something alone, anything at all, eventually it fell toward chaos. But I thought of hell as a fixed thing: a carousel in the worst of all possible worlds, where nothing could get better. All this time, we hadn't even been talking about the same thing. And what was so funny about the whole situation was that Constant had tried to tell me: in everything he had written, he'd pointed at this misunderstanding. I just didn't believe him, or I thought it was something we could overcome.

"Ocean," said Constant, in such a way I opened my eyes to look at him. That was how I acted around him—like I couldn't help myself. I looked up and he was there, beautiful and sharp, the only thing in focus. His cheekbones and his crooked mouth and his sideways nose. I could have drawn him from memory with the wrong hand. How long could you love someone? How did you stop? He was leaning over me, his hands braced against the side of the train car. If I could have reached, I would have kissed him. I would have kissed him and stopped caring about the rest of it, and he would have kissed me back.

"Come on," said Constant, and handed me a can of spray paint. "Come paint the last line."

I took it. The can was sticky and nearly empty. I was still shivering so hard the pea chattered against the aluminum like teeth. Constant and I stood before his map, which spanned the whole side of the train car, curved top to dirty bottom, the boroughs like continents, the rivers and roads. I was amazed again by how technically good it was, how clean each of his lines was, how sure his hands. I clutched the paint can tight with my frozen fingers.

"I don't know the G train route," I admitted.

I heard him shift his weight. "Here," he said. "Just follow me."

Then he leaned around me and began to trace a path on the map, his fingertip along the metal. I felt a stab of anxiety that I was about to ruin everything, and then I had to start painting anyway, because Constant was moving, showing me the way.

I followed Constant up and across Brooklyn, leaving

behind us an unsteady green line. When you looked at the map, it was obvious that someone, not the artist, had drawn the G line. But I couldn't turn back; there was nowhere else to go. On we went, into Queens.

"Here," said Constant. "Stop here."

It was so abrupt I covered his finger in lime-green paint. "Hey," he protested, and flicked me on the nose. I could feel the mark he left at the tip of it: wet, then drying. My heart seemed to swell wildly while the rest of my body seized. I wished I didn't feel such absurd and disproportionate things, just because he was near me. I wished I had fallen forward on the water tower, and we had never met.

"Constant," I began, just as he opened his mouth and said, "Listen, Ocean, I know I haven't been—"

All of a sudden we were hit by a beam of light. "Fuck," I heard Constant say, and then he shouted something else at me. I felt his hand on my wrist, and then it was gone. A wave of nausea had started in my gut and was spinning upward into my head, rocking me back. A dense gray tide of particles overtook me, even my eyeballs, with a rush and a speed that dislocated me from my body. For a moment I was afloat; then even my awareness was gone, and I was nothing at all.

JUDGMENT DAY

Ocean, come on, run. That was what Constant had shouted. Then I was waking up like I was being lifted out of water, toward light. Someone was shining a flashlight straight into my eyes. I flinched. I felt the light all the way through my brainstem, like a shock to the nape of my neck. Someone was prodding me harshly on the side of my face.

"Ma'am," someone was saying. "Ma'am, are you on any substances you'd like to tell us about? Ma'am."

My head was spinning. Even with my eyes closed, I kept seeing bursts of light that made me dizzy. I was sure I was going to faint again. I kept trying to swallow, to keep the feeling down. I could feel the wobble of the earth on its axis. I had no idea where I was. I couldn't believe how dizzy I felt. It felt like my entire body was moving rapidly in circles, whipping all my weight to the top of my head. I couldn't even say which way I was facing, or which way was up.

"Ma'am," someone was still saying. "Ma'am."

"I'm really light-headed," I managed to say. The treachery of words. My head wasn't light but extraordinarily heavy. I had no way of telling them how I felt. I didn't even know who they were.

I had fainted again. I curled myself around this realization, trying to reorient myself. It really felt like I had just died. It was exactly how I had felt at the top of the water tower.

Someone was hauling me to my feet. I knew I was going to vomit. My upper arm was in a vise grip—it really hurt. Then I was standing, my feet flat on some surface.

I opened my eyes. I was staring at a gun, which was attached to a policeman. His partner had me by the arm. Immediately I started dry-heaving. If I had anything in my stomach, I would have puked it up on their feet.

"Ma'am," the police officer said again, giving me a hard shake. I blinked. The train lot had been flooded with light, and I could see Constant's map in all its glory, and the wobbly green line of the G train, the same paint that was on my face and hands. For the first time, I saw the security camera fixed on the other side of the lot, under a bubble of black glass so there was no way to see where it was pointed, or to make it out in the dark.

Constant was gone. There were two officers, but they were both occupied with me. In the background was an MTA employee who must have called them, and an empty police cruiser. Constant was nowhere to be seen, gone like he'd never been there. The officer dug his hand into my biceps. *He wouldn't leave me,* I thought. *Run,* he had said. Maybe he was hiding beneath the train, about to jump out and save me. Maybe he was already in the police cruiser. I felt this terrible hope that this was true, that he had been arrested already and I just couldn't see him. *He wouldn't leave me.*

I started to cry. The officer holding me told me to turn around and patted me down. I flinched when he touched me. The handcuffs came around my bare wrists, pinning them behind me. I was shaking so violently my vision was blurry.

Constant had deserted me, and he had left his map unfinished on the side of the train. Neither thing seemed like him, I thought, and then I remembered: I didn't even know him.

It was bizarre how breaking even a small law meant losing all your rights. In the back of the police cruiser, dazed, that was all I could think about. The sharp ridges of the handcuffs dug into the delicate skin of my wrists. I had never even gotten detention before—I felt really emotionally unequipped for my circumstance. I remembered descending beneath the city with Constant on the night we met, how it had seemed impossible we were in the developed world, in the indomitable West. Now I couldn't believe it was the twenty-first century.

Constant left me, I thought. *He left me, he left me.* I thought it a thousand times, and it still didn't seem true. But I was alone in the back of the police cruiser, behind a wire mesh partition, my hands behind my back. Because of Constant.

At the precinct, everything was gray and dull. It was the ugliest place I had ever been. They took my coat and everything in it, and recorded all the information on my license. I watched them with a sinking feeling. That was it—there was my name in the system. I had no real idea what that meant, but I was full of foreboding.

"I'm not on drugs," I said, exhausted, when they asked for the tenth time. "Really, I'm not." They asked more questions. They asked me my name and looked skeptical when I told them. They wanted my address and my birthday and my social security number. I felt reduced to numbers. At the same time, I felt lost in my head, uncontained, like I was still falling.

At last they ushered me through a door to a room with a pair of cells in it. One was empty. In I went.

"Wait," I said, remembering suddenly, "don't I get a call?"

But the door had already shut behind the officer. Inside the cell there was an extraordinarily grimy bench, which I stayed resolutely away from for about two minutes before I all but collapsed onto it, curling my knees beneath my chin. I was shivering—it was really cold, like the heat wasn't even on. I hadn't been able to feel my ears in hours.

And then there was nothing to do but think. I had fainted

again. I had fainted *backward*—I could feel the bruise forming on the back of my head, tender when I prodded it. Could it have happened twice? Now I was supposed to be grateful, I thought, for life.

I thought about Constant, who had left me. I thought about him with my whole chest seizing. I thought about my mother, who loved me. I wondered what extreme lengths she had gone to by now, if she had called the school and learned that I had no dorm room or classes or professors, and put out an Amber Alert. I thought about how the school might revoke my acceptance now that I had been arrested. Probably my life was ruined. I thought about Georgie and Tashya, who didn't even know where I was, who would never imagine that I was here, in jail.

I thought about time and trains. I thought about language and meaning. I thought about entropy and the sea. I thought about how all of those things had become irreversibly tangled up with Constant, and how Constant had become irreversibly tangled up with me.

Hours later, the officer came back and motioned me out of the cell. I had to be fingerprinted, he explained, and then I could make my call.

The phone was the first landline I'd seen in a decade. For a moment I hesitated. I knew I should call my mother, who was probably making herself sick with worry—but the idea of dialing her number made me so anxious my throat closed. I was relieved not to have Constant's number, even after all this time. I would have called him; I wouldn't have been able to help myself.

I dialed. The phone rang for a long time. I was already panicking that I had wasted my call when at last Georgie answered.

"Hello?" she said, groggy.

"Georgie?" My voice shook.

"Ocean?" she shrieked. "Oh my god. Oh my god, Ocean, where are you? Tashya, wake up, it's Ocean! Where are you? Why did my phone say this was a blocked number? I can't believe you just disappeared! We were so worried. Where are you? Are you with your philosopher? You haven't been kidnapped, have you?"

I glanced at the police officer. "Yes," I said. "Well . . . I sort of got kind of arrested."

"What? What did you say?"

"I'm in jail," I said, louder. Then I started to cry. "Can you call Benny's mom and tell her I can't tutor him tomorrow?"

"What?" Georgie said again. In the background, I could hear Tashya saying, "What, what, what did she say?" Georgie shushed her. "You got *what*? You're *where*?"

"In jail," I said. I hated my voice when I was crying.

"Oh my god," said Georgie. "Oh my god. What the fuck. Okay. Okay, oh my god, Tash—"

"Ocean?" Tashya had taken the phone. "Ocean, what happened?"

My throat was closing fast. "I . . ." I took a shaky breath. "I don't know." I didn't know where to start. The cemetery felt so long ago. The night seemed to span years, and its events disparate, like they had happened to different people, none of them quite me. "Tashya, I'm in jail."

"In jail," said Tashya slowly. "In jail. Okay. Where? In which precinct?"

I told her. I could hear her mulling; I could hear the exact expression on her face. Georgie was breathing heavily in the background, crying, "Oh my god!" and uttering every expletive in the book. All of a sudden I missed them both so much it was like my heart was leaping out of my chest. I started crying harder. "Tash, I shouldn't have left tonight. I should have stayed home with you guys. Did you get the pizza? Was it good?"

I couldn't express how badly I wanted them to have gotten the pizza, and for it to have been the best pizza. In my bones, in my marrow, I could see how differently this night could have gone—it was almost like a memory, the way I could see it so clearly.

"Ocean?" said Tashya. "Can you take a breath for me? Seriously, right now. Take a deep breath."

I did. It did help, until I dared a glance at the police officer, who looked impatient. I wondered if there was a time limit on the single call you got when you were arrested.

"Okay," said Tashya. "Okay. The philosopher . . . he's with you?"

I squeezed my eyes shut. I couldn't speak for several seconds. "No," I whispered.

Then I was glad it was Tashya on the phone, instead of Georgie. Georgie would have questions; Georgie would have called him names, threatened murder, made me cry. Tashya only paused, and said, "Okay. Listen, we're going to figure this out, okay? It's going to be okay."

"Benny's mom," I sobbed.

"Yeah, we'll call her too. Ocean, you're okay? Can you tell me you're okay?"

"Tash, do you think I'm dead? Do you think I died and went to hell? Do you think I'm literally in hell?"

"No," said Tashya flatly. "Georgie and I are here too, and we're definitely not in hell. We're going to get you out of there, okay? Okay?"

"Okay," I whispered. "Okay."

"It's going to be okay," she said again. And then that was it. I hung up. Putting the phone back in its cradle was like losing my final grip on reality; I retreated back into the haze of my mind, where nothing seemed quite real, and everything was far away. The police officer returned me to my cell and closed the door firmly behind me. I wondered who had invented the very first lock; I wondered if there was any real difference between keeping something *in* and trying to keep other people *out*.

Eventually even my anxiety settled into boredom. I was there for a long, long time. This thing, time. I couldn't escape it or make it go faster, I could only wait as it carried me forward. I thought about how I had fainted, how it had felt. It *was* awful to be conscious here in the cell, but the sickening sensation of my own consciousness leaving me was worse. It was the first time I had ever thought anything like that.

Eventually they put me in a van to the courthouse for arraignment. That was what they told me, anyway—I wasn't sure what it meant, or where exactly I was going. Outside, the sun was rising. I watched the rosy light illuminate Brooklyn, the buildings rising golden as we drove downtown. In the front of the police van, two officers were talking about their weekend plans: they were both taking their families on separate trips to Vermont. Their lives were normal; in my life, everything was crumbling. We were only a few feet apart, but we were all stuck in our own worlds.

It took a really long time to get into the courthouse. There were so many locks and procedures. At different stages my handcuffs were exchanged for other handcuffs, or taken off, then put back on again. For the first time in hours I saw other people. They were almost all men, the police as well the people they had arrested, and I had never felt so small, not even when I stood next to Constant. It was hard to tell who was just angry and who was dangerous—especially since the police treated everyone like they were dangerous, even me. I was pretty sure I wasn't dangerous, though it felt like my brain was seeping like poison out of my ears. I had no idea what was going on, or even what day it was. I hadn't eaten or slept in what felt like a lifetime.

I was handed off to different officers, then different officers again. At some point I had my mug shot taken. As the camera flashed, I felt like I was watching all of this happen to someone else. This was the dead feeling, this detachment from my body. I was so tired I felt like I was floating, tugged along with my hands tied behind my back. If I got through this, I promised myself I would drink more water, eat regularly, never faint again. I wouldn't hurt myself or anyone else, if I could just get out of here and go home to my own bed, and sleep for five years straight.

Beneath the courthouse, I shared a holding cell with fifteen or twenty other women. For hours, no one spoke to me or even looked in my direction. There was a single pro-bono lawyer seeing people before their arraignments. It took a really long time because the lawyer kept disappearing—it turned out that she was also juggling cases upstairs, before the judge. Inside the cell, the other women grew periodically agitated and called her names every time she had to leave.

All of the benches were occupied. I didn't want to sit on

the ground, so I leaned against a tiny ledge by the wall of bars and tried not to touch anything. The cell looked like it had never been cleaned, though it smelled heavily of bleach. I figured I would be there for a long time, since everyone else had arrived there before me. A guard came and handed milk cartons and cheese sandwiches through the bars. I declined both, though I hadn't eaten since before Tashya's concert, because I didn't have a Lactaid pill and the cell had only a metal toilet in full view.

At some point we all went around the cell and shared what we had been arrested for. Most of the women were there on drug possession charges. One woman had been near a bar fight—not even in it. One of the girls was only sixteen. She had been at a party that got busted after a noise complaint, and she was the only one who had gotten arrested, though many of the boys had been far more belligerent. "Everyone else at the party was white," she said, by way of explanation, and no one was surprised. In the cell, only one woman was white. She had been on the floor the entire time, sleeping off something that made her scream incoherently once every half hour.

"Vandalization," I said in a tiny voice, when it was my turn. "I spray-painted a train."

"Really?" someone said. "What's your tag?"

Then I had to explain that I didn't have a tag at all—it was the first time I'd ever painted anything. "I was with . . . a friend." I swallowed hard.

"Well, so what's his tag?"

"He paints maps," I said. "Subway maps."

The woman snorted. "You're kidding," she said. "All that trouble for a subway map?"

At first I was offended on Constant's behalf. But she wasn't the only one scoffing. It was true that Constant's maps didn't really fit with the rest of the street art I had seen. In fact, they were so different they seemed almost inconsiderate of what street art *was*, as a culture—like, who was Constant to think his maps were better than the ones that were already available everywhere, and who was he to go around vandalizing property whenever he wanted? Why did he even go through so much trouble to paint them—what was the point? If *meaning* was the same thing as *use*, was there any value in a map no one saw?

"Ocean? Sun?"

I was so startled I nearly fell off my ledge. My name came tinnily from the loudspeaker in the lawyer's vestibule, but the voice was new and male. My legs had fallen asleep, and I had to shuffle across the cell. I let myself in. In the vestibule, there was a dirty partition between us, and we had to speak into an intercom, the way you would receive a visitor in prison.

"Ocean," he said. He wasn't much older than me, but he was past the age divide that made him a different species—twenty-five or twenty-six, a real adult. I felt acutely self-conscious of how messy my life was. "Hi. I'm Russell, I'm from Harold Szabo's office."

"You emailed our landlord," I realized, remembering his name. And then my stomach sank. "Harold knows you're here?"

"No," said Russell the lawyer. "Georgie called me directly. I usually do a pro-bono shift on weekends in Manhattan, but I live right in the Seaport."

I considered this. It was so strange how language worked— that anyone understood each other at all. He was telling me he lived in the Seaport because the trek to Brooklyn wasn't much out of the way for him, like I hadn't terribly inconvenienced him. It seemed as though we left at least half of all communication to subtext. I sighed. Maybe that was why Russell was a lawyer, and I was in jail. In law, they left nothing to subtext.

Russell explained what was happening for the first time. I had to be arraigned before the judge for two misdemeanors: vandalizing property, and also holding the spray paint can I had used to vandalize. I wasn't sure why these were two separate charges, but I didn't interrupt to ask. He went on. He was sure I would get some light service to the community. Probably I'd have to go back to the train yard and power wash the train. In six months, if I didn't get in any other kind of trouble, the incident would be expunged from my records, and I'd never even have to tell anyone about it.

"I'm surprised they bothered to arrest you," he said, shuffling through papers. "Normally they'd probably just slap you with a ticket—ah, I see. The officers were finishing up a shift." He said this in a significant way, and then looked at me like I should know what that meant.

"What does that mean?" I asked.

Russell stood up. "Officers are more inclined to perform an arrest at the end of a shift," he said. "They have to stay and write up the booking paperwork, and then they get paid overtime. All right, Ocean. I'm going to get these filed upstairs, and then I'm going to check in with the other lawyer who's been down here and ask if she wants me to take a few of her cases. She seems to have a lot on her plate."

For some reason, I felt even heavier and sadder than I had before, though now the end was within sight. I understood why Constant had run away. Constant—and everyone else, it seemed—understood something that I didn't: that the world did not consist of safety nets but traps. There were all these systems that worked against us despite what they purported. I remembered Constant's face, when he first stepped into the light at Green-Wood—how he had looked at me, with astonishment. I thought about how he had held my whole head in his palm, after he lifted me over the bars of the gate.

"Your friend," the woman in the cell said. "He's in here too?"

"No," I said. Several other women raised their heads and began to pay attention. "He . . . he got away."

The first woman let out a long, low whistle. "Damn," she said. "Bet you want to kill him."

I did, a little. I wanted him out of my life so badly I wished he'd never been born, that I'd never met him, that I hadn't agreed to let him walk me home the night all the lights went out, that I hadn't slept with him, that I had never written back. The problem was that he was still the one I wanted to talk to about all this, about jail and bureaucracy and failed systems, even though I knew he wouldn't listen properly, and would probably only respond with something he'd read about Foucault.

Everyone, even the lady sprawled on the ground, was looking at me sympathetically, like they all understood. Probably everyone knew how it felt to be fucked over, or to like someone more than they liked you. This made me feel worse, not better. It was terrible to be a girl in the world. I had never felt more pathetic.

If I ever saw him again, I told myself, I would tell him everything. How small he made me feel, and how I couldn't stand it anymore. I would tell him to stop writing to me, and I would leave him alone. I repeated it, for conviction. Nonetheless what stuck in my head was *if I ever see him again.* I was extraordinarily sad.

•••

At last a guard came to extract me from the holding cell. Again we went up and down so many flights of stairs I lost all sense of direction until, at last, the officer led us through a door to the courtroom, and I saw natural light for the first time since I had been transported to the courthouse. It was already sunset; almost a whole day had passed.

The mood was solemn. The only person talking was Russell, standing before the judge, who sat at a great height and looked bored. The officer directed both of us to a pew, where three other people in handcuffs were already sitting and fidgeting. When I tried to sit, I understood why. There was no way to get comfortable on a wooden pew with your hands behind your back.

When it was my turn, an officer led me before the podium, and remained beside me so I couldn't run off. It was really humiliating to stand there like that, being looked down upon. It seemed to me that the justice system could be a little less heavy-handed about power dynamics—so much seemed to rely on the symbols of authority and justice, rather than the real thing. The longer I stood there, the more it all began to seem malicious, from the judge's predatory height to the jargon no one but Russell could understand, as though it was all there to make me feel smaller than I was.

Russell read the charges aloud. The judge looked at me the whole time. I squirmed, unable to meet her gaze. Russell read the recommended sentence: that I would have to wash the train clean, after which my records would be expunged in six months. Then I didn't care about justice, as a system, anymore. I only wanted to be free of it—I only wanted to get out of there, and have it wiped from memory.

"Do you consent to perform service to the community?" the judge intoned.

I nodded.

"I need verbal confirmation," she said impatiently.

I swallowed. "Yes," I squeaked out.

And that was it. She nodded and signed something. Before I knew what was going on, the officer unlocked my handcuffs, and my shoulders popped back to where they were meant to be. Russell came over and explained in rapid, low tones that I was free to go. He would email the train yard on my behalf and set up a time for my community service. Once again my head was spinning—everything was happening distantly outside of me again. And then he turned his attention to the next case, and there was nothing for me to do but leave.

I went out the main door of the courtroom. I got a brief impression of a grand hall held up by grimy columns, built in an era when we still taxed billionaires to build public structures, like jails.

Then Georgie was flying at me, shrieking, with Tashya close behind. There must have been a moment of impact, but the next thing I knew, Georgie was hanging on to me, and Tashya was patting my face.

"Are you okay?" Tashya was saying. "Tell me you're okay." It was hard to hear her over Georgie.

"Down with policing!" Georgie shouted. Five different officers looked our way. She waggled her sweatshirt at them, which featured Porky Pig in uniform shooting himself in the foot.

"Georgie, Jesus," said Tashya. "Ocean, seriously, you're okay? Here." She handed me a bottle of water, like it wasn't the best present I'd ever received.

"I'm okay," I reassured them after chugging the water down. "I'm okay."

And then I wasn't. There he was. That was what it was to love someone, I realized, as everything else fell away. I saw him clearly. I could see that he was sorry. I could see that he cared about me. I could see that he was worried about me. *Constantine.* He was standing by the doors. Now he started toward us, his coat flapping, his body moving through time.

"Ocean," he said.

My throat closed. My hands went clammy.

Georgie whipped around. Her eyes narrowed upon him. *"You,"* she said.

"All right," said Tashya, and towed her away. She threw

a look back at me. I swallowed hard. I nodded at her. I felt such a rush of fondness for both of them: Georgie, who would slap anyone in the world on my behalf, and Tashya, who trusted me to know what to do. "I'm okay," I mouthed at her. I was okay, even though I was alone, and now I was alone with him.

I could only look at our feet. My dirty winter boots and his wet sneakers, facing each other on the ancient linoleum. My whole body felt tender. I could feel him looking at me. I was worried my nose would start bleeding. *Jump, jump.* The instinct was thick like phlegm in my lungs.

"Ocean," he said again. I had to squeeze my eyes closed to keep from crying. He said it like the first time he had ever said it, when I told him my name in the dark. *Ocean, Ocean.* Like an incantation, like none of this was real. Like I could stop the next thing from happening.

"Constantine," I said.

And then, already, there was nothing else to say.

"I'm sorry," he said. He said it in a rush, like he was desperate. "I thought you were right behind me. I didn't even realize you weren't until I was at the train station. I was still talking to you as I was swiping through the turnstile, I swear to god. I didn't realize—I should have checked, I didn't think. . . ."

I'd never seen him so rattled.

"I'm sorry," he said again. I looked at him. His long

eyelashes. His crooked mouth beneath his crooked nose. *Constant.* My whole body hurt.

"Hey," he said. "I brought this for you."

He rummaged in his coat and pulled out my copy of *The Little Prince.* For a second I could only stare at it; then I realized he meant for me to take it, and I scrambled. Our hands touched. I nearly unraveled. I still couldn't talk.

"Thank you," he said, after a beat. "For letting me borrow it."

"Sure," I whispered.

"Are you okay? Are you cold?" he asked. "What happened to your coat?"

I wrapped my arms around myself. "It's at the precinct," I said. "How did you know to come here?"

"Just did some research," he said. "Look, Ocean, I'm sorry you had to go through that. I went right back when I realized you weren't with me, but I saw that they already had you in handcuffs. I called all the precincts in the area, and found out you'd be at central booking. I didn't think it would take so long—I couldn't believe you hadn't come out yet. . . ."

My ears were ringing. Constant kept going about how they never should have held me for so long, but I couldn't hear anything else he said. *They already had you in handcuffs.*

"You watched them take me away," I said.

He stopped in the middle of a sentence about his theory of

justice, which had something to do with free will. Everything was suddenly quiet.

"I . . ." He ran a hand through his hair. "I . . . yeah, I made it back when they were putting you in the cruiser. Were you okay? You're okay now? Maybe it was the light, but your face was green."

He had come back. Somehow hearing this was worse, though I knew that wasn't exactly fair to him. Obviously there was nothing he could have done. I glanced at Tashya, still keeping hold of Georgie, who was glaring at Constant. I knew, with my entire being, that neither of them would have just hung back while policemen put me in a cruiser. There was nothing they could have done either, but neither would have stood back and watched. I knew it; I knew them.

I closed my eyes. There was nothing I could say to him. You couldn't make someone stick their neck out for you, especially when the police were involved. You couldn't make people love you: they did, or they didn't. There were so many things I was powerless to change. The justice system and the education system and my mother's mind and how Constant felt about me, or how he defined friendship, or what we owed each other.

"Ocean," he said. "I'm sorry. I really am."

For what? I shook my head and clutched my book. I wanted things to get better, not worse.

"I think you should go," I whispered.

For the first time since I had known him, Constant had nothing to say. I could see him struggling, his mouth going straight, then crooked, then straight again. I felt a rush of affection for him that almost made me say, "No, wait, stay." I felt the words on my tongue; I barely caught them between my teeth. I wanted him to go. I wanted this day to be over.

"We shouldn't write to each other anymore," I made myself say.

For a moment, I was sure he would protest. My whole body was tense, waiting for him to say he would write to me anyway, always—but he let out an enormous breath and nodded. I would never forget the way his face looked at that moment.

"Okay," he said. He gathered himself, straightening; he grew even taller. "Okay," he said again, more quietly. "I'll just go catch a train." He looked at me. The qing of his eyes. He gave me a last grin, or the ghost of one. I could feel the tears welling; I needed him to go, I couldn't bear another second. I closed my eyes.

"Ocean," he said. *Say it again,* I thought. *Again and again.*

When I opened my eyes, he was gone.

ARIADNE'S SCARF

Georgie called a rideshare and we headed to the precinct to get my stuff. At first I was grateful to have her and Tashya with me, but then Georgie spent the whole ride insulting Constantine, when all I wanted was to forget I had ever met him. Then, at the precinct, she was so aggressive to the officers that they almost refused to let us in.

"How could you take her coat?" she yelled through the plexiglass partition. "It's below zero outside, you assholes!"

Eventually they let me in, by myself. At the desk, another officer wanted to see my ID in order to return my possessions.

"But," I said, "you have my ID. You have my whole wallet."

"Well, you need to come back with a second ID."

Immediately I started crying. I couldn't believe this bullshit. How was I supposed to produce a second ID when they had my whole wallet? What was I supposed to do, come all the way back with my passport? I was so exhausted I could barely keep my eyes open.

"Just check her face against the ID," said a second officer. I looked up. I had to wipe my eyes several times to see. It was the same policeman who had arrested me. He wouldn't meet my eyes. The clerk went to rummage around the back room and returned with my stuff in a plastic bag, along with a packet of paper detailing every single thing they had taken from me, from all of the cards in my wallet to the loose jewelry and change in my coat pocket.

The last thing they gave back to me was Constant's scarf. It still smelled like him. There was a trash can right by the door. I knew I shouldn't keep it.

"Stay out of trouble," the officer said to me. I knew I was dismissed. I put on my coat. I hesitated, and then put on the scarf too. It was awfully cold out.

Then we were home, and I had to call my mother. The five minutes during which I sat beside my charging phone, waiting for it to turn on, were almost worse than all the hours I'd spent in jail combined. There was this problem, with parents. I knew I had treated my mother badly, but I didn't know how to fix it, or how to stop.

When I was three or four, my mother had spent an entire paycheck on a camcorder and set about documenting the most mortifying moments of my childhood. The VHS tapes piled up beneath the TV console, until the home videos outnumbered real movies, and we had to keep extra boxes on the bookshelf. Whenever she got mad at me, I knew I could make her forgive me by playing a tape of myself as a baby, especially one where I was speaking Chinese. Even now, just thinking about it made me feel tender with guilt. How vulnerable it was to love someone like that! And how painful, to be loved! Eventually the VHS player broke, and we moved the tapes to the basement.

Tashya had gone to bed. Georgie told me, in low tones, that earlier Tashya had gotten a call from the conservatory saying she had been awarded second place in the competition. Tashya was so crushed that even Georgie knew better than to bother her. "Thomas Sato didn't win, either," Georgie assured me. "The trombone player won, with the bowl cut, remember? Can you believe it? Anyway, Thomas Sato got *fourth*. He was only an honorable mention." It was little consolation.

I stared at my laptop, also charging on my bed. My limbs moved of their own accord, faster than my spinning mind. I crossed the room and opened my computer. The document was already there, waiting on the screen.

I couldn't breathe. The whole thing was blank, except for the map. It was the only thing left. Constant had gotten there before me.

My phone began to buzz furiously. At first I thought it was only my notifications coming back to life, but it was my mother. Like she could sense an opportunity—or like she had been trying nonstop.

My hands shook. I was literally going to puke. I almost couldn't answer it, but I had to—she would only call again.

I picked up. "Mama?"

"Sun Haiying," she burst out, and then she started sobbing, and couldn't say anything for a long time. I didn't know what to do. I was mortified to hear her crying. I tried several times to ask her what was wrong, but I felt like such an asshole I couldn't get it out.

After several minutes, she managed to say, "Are you okay? Where have you been?"

Relief coursed through me. At least she didn't know I had been in jail. "I'm okay," I said, which was the truth even if it didn't quite feel like it. "My phone broke. I'm sorry. I couldn't turn it on for a while."

"Oh," said my mother, taking that in. I could almost hear all of the drastic scenarios she had concocted for herself in the last twenty hours dissolving. It occurred to me that maybe all of my anxiety had come from her.

And then she came for me. "I got an email from your school," she said. "It said you weren't a student there this year, and you had to declare your intent to attend next semester if you wanted to keep your acceptance and your scholarships. I called the office, and they said the same thing. They said you deferred."

I swallowed. "It's true."

That was when she began to yell. What the hell had I been thinking? What did this even mean? Had I been lying to her this entire time? How could I have deferred—didn't I know that education was the most important thing? On and on she went. It was actually preferable to the crying. The worst was already over, I thought; then I froze, and thought it again.

The worst was over. It felt true to me—I recognized it to be true. Surely everything that could have gone wrong had already gone wrong, which meant everything was going to get better. I started shaking. I looked around my room, at the last of the light, and the dust motes swirling around in the golden hour.

I'm not in hell, I said to myself. That felt true too.

"Ocean?" said my mother. "Ocean, did you hear? I want you to come home, right now. I mean it. I'll come get you myself."

"Mama," I said. "I met a boy."

I met him on the train, I told her. It was the only way I could talk about Constant, because it was the only way I had known him: in transit. I could map out the whole length of time we had known each other, from the subway station to the C train in his dream to the ferry, the paragraphs I had written and read on the way to my tutoring appointments, the Q train to the beach and all the others I had cried on, and the last train, the sleeping train, the one we had painted. I told my mother how he was at my school, and how I thought that meant I could trust him. I told her that he was really smart, and liked to talk about gravity and wasps. I told her he was a philosopher, and a painter.

"This boy," said my mother, sounding suspicious, "he's older than you?"

I hesitated. "I mean, we would have been in school together. He's . . . he's graduating."

"Ocean," she said. "He's finishing a section of his life that you're only beginning."

I opened my mouth, then closed it. Constant had seemed to understand me, but maybe that was only because he had already gone through all the things that were plaguing me. He wasn't wiser—he was only older. Perhaps Constant had identified in me what Tashya and Georgie and everyone else could see plainly in my face: they all knew I was anxious about expressing myself. I was daunted by moving across the country and making friends. I was daunted by life, so I put it off a year, only that made it even worse, because I met Constant while I was adrift.

"I know," I managed. "I'm not going to see him again."

And I wouldn't. I still wanted to—I wanted him even though he didn't make me feel good about myself. But it would pass. That was the thing about this life: unbearable things come, and then they go. I marveled again at this realization, that I could recognize it as true. I wasn't Sisyphus, and I wasn't a wasp. I was still me, in this vast city, and I had better friends than Constantine.

"Good," huffed my mama. "Ocean, why didn't you go to school? It's a good school. You got accepted. How could you not go?"

"I . . ." I swallowed, then cleared my throat. "Mama, did anything . . . weird happen at that old water tower last summer?"

"The water tower?"

"I noticed they moved the ladder," I said. "That's all."

"The ladder?" She was quiet for a long time. "Have you climbed the water tower?"

Another long pause. "I'm okay," I said. I tried to make my voice reassuring. "I felt . . . overwhelmed. I needed some . . . space. And I feel more okay now."

It was ridiculous to say these things to my immigrant mother. I felt really tense, knowing she was probably about to become hysterical and tell me I was coddled and oversensitive. I *was* coddled and oversensitive. I didn't know how to explain to her what I felt in either English or Chinese. Suddenly she seemed so far away, like we didn't even know each other at all.

"I don't understand—" my mother tried.

"Mama," I said. "I'm not going to come home. I have to finish my lease here. I have a job tutoring, and I like my roommates. I'll go to school in the fall. I'll email the admissions office as soon as I'm done talking to you, okay? I promise. But . . . I need you to trust me. I can take care of this. Of—of myself. I just needed some time to figure it out. And . . . I'm not going to hurt myself. I swear." It was extraordinarily difficult to say even those lame few phrases to her.

The worst is over. I tried to remember this. "I feel . . . better now." I realized I meant it, or at least I did for the moment, and I would try to feel okay tomorrow.

She didn't say anything for almost a whole minute. I could tell she was crying again. I didn't know what to do with myself. I felt really guilty for just about everything.

"I love you," she said. She said it in Chinese, which startled me.

"I love you too," I managed.

"I want you to take care of yourself," she said.

"I will," I said.

"And drink more water."

"Okay."

"And sleep eight hours a day."

"Uh-huh."

"Don't talk to any more older boys."

"Okay."

"And I want you to call me tomorrow," she said. "Every day."

"Okay," I said. It was inconvenient, but it was the least I could do. "Okay, I'll call you."

"And you have to email the school," she said.

I almost laughed. I could feel the relief welling up my throat. "I can do that," I said. "I'll go do that now."

"Yes," she said. "Ocean. You'll come to me if you need help? If I can help you?"

I nodded. I realized that maybe my mother was in a unique position to understand exactly what I felt at that moment—I realized that she had probably made similar apologetic phone calls to my grandparents, from even farther away. It hurt my chest. It comforted me. "Yes, Mama, I'll come to you for help."

"Okay," she said. "I love you."

"I love you," I said, and ended the call. I was so exhausted that if I had collapsed on the bed I would have fallen asleep before my head hit the pillow, but I went back to my computer.

Before I could change my mind, I deleted the document from its folder. Since it was only shared with me, it disappeared immediately—there were no copies to root out.

It was gone. It was over.

I sent an email to the admissions office, saying I would attend in person in the fall. Georgie knocked on my door right as I was closing my laptop. She hung in my doorway and looked at me seriously.

"That's the way to do it," she said. "You have to have just one massive mental breakdown, and your parents will leave you alone."

She climbed into bed with me and held me while I cried. I fell asleep almost immediately.

EPILOGUE

Georgie ordered herself a stick-and-poke kit. She had decided her new calling in life was to become a tattoo artist. She gave herself a ring of tiny stars around her ankle, which turned out so well that I almost let her practice on me before Tashya stepped in and made me wait until Georgie wasn't high.

Spring came so gradually we didn't notice until we were sweating in our coats. Georgie had started reading a lot of books about climate change, and she talked almost nonstop about how the earth was soon to be uninhabitable, and we were living amid the sixth extinction. In any case, winter was over, and despite the bigger picture, we were all relieved that the wind no longer chafed our faces raw. Tashya started learning a new concerto, for next year's competition. Benny took his PSATs and aced them.

The day came to go back to the train yard and perform my service to the community. Georgie and Tashya came with me. On the subway down, Georgie kept talking about suicide. "I mean, evolutionarily, it makes sense that, you know, like . . . if you're badly adapted to your environment, your serotonin levels reflect that, and you self-select out." She drew a finger across her throat as Tashya mouthed, "Shut up!" when she thought I wasn't looking. But in fact I thought it was sort of a relief—to finally talk about it openly, and to have the right language. Georgie had taken it upon herself to destigmatize mental health, especially around me. So far she had given me a voucher for a free video session with her therapist, a book on psychedelics and depression, a sun lamp for seasonal affective disorder, and a family-sized bottle of vitamin D gummies that tasted like stone fruits.

"The problem is," Georgie continued, "then the environment started changing too quickly. The agricultural revolution made everyone a serf, then the industrial revolution made everyone a factory worker, and now no one is adapted to any environment, because every environment is artificial. No one's well adapted to anything, we're just all trying to off ourselves."

"Georgie," Tashya said.

"What?" said Georgie. She linked her arm through mine. "I'm just saying. Anyway, sixth extinction and all. Did you know that almost all the frogs are dead?"

The train yard looked really different during the day. The light made everything uglier and revealed all the weeds and loose trash. Georgie was delighted. "This place is so *weird*," she said, again and again. We found an MTA worker, who apparently had no idea we were meant to be there. I explained to her the situation—how I had vandalized a train and was here to clean it and fulfill my community service.

"But these trains don't need to be cleaned," she said, baffled. "They've been retired—they're headed for the ocean, to become artificial reefs."

"No way," said Georgie. Her face was shining like this was the most wonderful thing she'd ever heard. She started asking a lot of questions. It turned out the train cars were to be stripped of their stainless steel, loaded onto barges, and then dropped along the Eastern seaboard, to become habitats for marine life. I watched Georgie, talking so easily, and I realized what it meant to understand someone: it was to see the world as they saw it. Georgie saw everyone as interesting, so even when they intimidated her, she still found them worth her time. That was why Georgie could win over just about anyone, and could find a way to talk to them. Tashya saw everyone as reasonable—even Thomas Sato had his motivations.

But I saw everyone as dead, which was to say I thought of them as props in my own life, like no one else was real at all. That was the root of all my problems; it was why I was so prone to loneliness. Constant saw everyone as lost, which was how he had found me.

"Anyway," said the MTA employee. "You see that there's no real point to cleaning them."

"But didn't the court contact you?" Tashya asked. "To make sure this was okay, as community service?"

The MTA employee snorted. "Honey, if anyone in this city knew how to communicate, we could save a billion dollars a day."

I nodded along—I thought communication was valuable too. "But the thing is," I said, "I still have to do my community service."

"Look," she said, sighing. "Why don't you girls pick up some trash, and then we'll see what else there is for you to do?"

Luckily, there was a lot of trash in the train yard. "Most of the city is built on landfill," said Georgie, and started rattling neighborhoods off as we gathered trash bags and gloves: Battery Park City, Canarsie, big chunks of Ellis Island and Staten Island. "They built Ellis Island with all the dirt they excavated when they were digging the subways," she said. I made a note to suggest she try leading groups of tourists through Manhattan, when she got tired of tattooing.

We filled several bags with trash. Our hands got dirty, despite the gloves. The trains in the yard weren't the same ones Constant and I had painted—I looked for his map, but it was already under the sea. The wind smelled so promising that I would have stayed out there for longer, but the train yard wasn't huge, and eventually we ran out of stuff to pick up. We stacked our bags by the guard vestibule and admired them: destined for landfill, and then remade.

The MTA employee poked her head out. "Good work, girls. I'd say the community has been served." She waved me off when I tried to protest. "Go on."

Tashya and Georgie looked at me. "Now what?" said Georgie.

I shrugged. "Well," I said. "I guess we should get back on the subway."